"十三五"国家重点出版规划项目

李白诗歌全集英译
A Complete Edition of Pai Li's Poems in Chinese and English
With Annotations

赵彦春 译·注
Translated and Annotated by Yanchun Chao

第三卷
Volume III

上海大学出版社
·上海·

卷 三

目 录
Contents

- 499 **古近体诗五十三首**
  Old-new Rhythmic Poetry, 53 Poems

- 501 秋浦歌十七首
  A Song of Autumn Shore, 17 Poems

- 519 当涂赵炎少府粉图山水歌
  Viewing a Painting at Tangt'u, in the House of Yan Chao, a Constable

- 522 永王东巡歌十一首
  Prince E'er on East March, 11 Poems

- 533 上皇西巡南京歌十首
  His Majesty's Tour West to the Southern Town, Ten Poems

- 543 峨眉山月歌
  A Song of the Moon o'er Mt. Brow

- 544 峨眉山月歌送蜀僧晏入中京
  A Song of the Moon o'er Mt. Brow to Yan, a Monk from Shu, Who Comes to Capital

- 546 赤壁歌送别
  Farewell at Red Wall

- 548 江夏行
  In Riversummer

- 551 怀仙歌
  A Song of Immortals

- 552 玉真仙人词
  A Lyric for Princess Jade

554	清溪行	
	A Clean Brook	
555	酬殷明佐见赠五云裘歌	
	Thanks to Mingts'o Yin for His Gift of Five Cloud Fur	
558	临路歌	
	A Roc Song	
560	古意	
	Feeling the Past	
562	山鹧鸪词	
	Hill Partridges	
564	历阳壮士勤将军名思齐歌	
	A Song of General Ch'in, a Gallant from Leeshine	
566	草书歌行	
	A Song of Cursive Script	
569	和卢侍御通塘曲	
	A Poem of Tung Pond in Reply to Vice Imperial Inspector	

573　**古近体诗四十三首**
Old-new Rhythmic Poetry, 43 Poems

575	赠孟浩然	
	To Haojan Meng	
576	赠从兄襄阳少府皓	
	To My Cousin, County Inspector of Sowshine	
578	淮海对雪赠傅霭	
	Singing in Snow to Ai Fu in Huaihai	
580	赠徐安宜	
	To Hsu, the Magistrate of Peace	
582	赠任城卢主簿潜	
	To Secretary Lu of Jen	
584	早秋赠裴十七仲堪	
	To Chung K'an P'ei Seventeen in Early Autumn	

587	赠范金卿二首
	To Fan, the Magistrate, Two Poems
590	赠瑕丘王少府
	To Wang, a Sheriff of Spotknoll
592	东鲁见狄博通
	Seeing Broadcom Ti in East Lu
593	见京兆韦参军量移东阳二首
	Seeing Staff Wei Moved from Capital to Eastshine, Two Poems
595	赠丹阳横山周处士惟长
	To Staff Chou in the Broadwise Hills in Redshine
597	玉真公主别馆苦雨赠卫尉张卿二首
	Two Poems to Royal Captain Chang at Princess Jade True's Villa in a Rain
602	赠韦秘书子春
	To Secretary Sirspring Wei
605	赠韦侍御黄裳二首
	To Yellowrobe Wei, the Royal Servant, Two Poems
608	赠薛校书
	To Hsüeh, a Book Compiler
610	赠何七判官昌浩
	To Boom Ho Seven, a Military Judge
612	读诸葛武侯传书怀赠长安崔少府叔封昆季
	To Ts'ui, a Sheriff in the Capital When Reading Bright Chuke's Book
615	赠郭将军
	To General Kuo
616	驾去温泉后赠杨山人
	To Yang, a Hermit, After Accompanying His Majesty to Flora Pool
618	温泉侍从归逢故人
	Meeting My Friend When I Come Back from Royal Hunting
619	赠裴十四
	To P'ei Fourteen

621	赠崔侍御	
	To Ts'ui, the Royal Servant	
623	述德兼陈情上哥舒大夫	
	Reporting to Marshal Han Koshu	
625	雪谗诗赠友人	
	Beware of Slander, to My Friend	
631	赠参寥子	
	To Sir Silence	
633	赠饶阳张司户燧	
	To Sui Chang, a Household Registrar in Richshine	
635	赠清漳明府侄聿	
	To Yü, My Nephew, Magistrate of Clearflow	
639	赠临洺县令皓弟	
	To Brother Hao, Magistrate of Linming	
640	赠郭季鹰	
	To Eagle Kuo	
641	邺中赠王大,劝入高凤石门山幽居	
	To Firstborn Wang from Mid-Yeh, Whom I Advise to Retire to Hiphoenix's Mt. Stone Gate	
644	赠华州王司士	
	To Wang, an Organization Official from Flora	
645	赠卢征君昆弟	
	To Lu Brothers, Recruits	
647	赠新平少年	
	To the Young Man in New Peace	
649	赠崔侍御	
	To Ts'ui, the Royal Servant	
651	走笔赠独孤驸马	
	To Adjunct Groom Loneliness	
653	赠嵩山焦炼师	
	To the Woman Alchemist on Mt. Tower	
657	口号赠杨征君	
	An Oral Impromptu to Yang, a Recruit	

658	上李邕 To Yung Li	
660	赠张公洲革处士 To Ke, a Clerk from Chang's Shoal	
663	**古近体诗二十四首** Old-new Rhythmic Poetry, 24 Poems	
665	秋日炼药院镊白发,赠元六兄林宗 To Lintsung Yüan Six, Sighing o'er Gray Hair at Concoction Yard on an Autumn Day	
668	书情赠蔡舍人雄 To Secretary Man Tsai	
673	忆襄阳旧游赠马少府巨 To Chü Ma, My Old Friend in Sowshine, a County Sheriff	
675	对雪献从兄虞城宰 To My Cousin, Mayor of Yü, a Verse Written in Snow	
676	访道安陵遇盖还为余造真箓,临别留赠 To Huan Kai Who, Made a Wordist Figure for Me in Peaceridge	
680	赠崔郎中宗之 To Secretary Tsungchih Ts'ui	
682	赠崔咨议 To Ts'ui, a Consultant	
684	赠昇州王使君忠臣 To Loyal Wang, a Civil Governor of Sunrise	
686	赠别从甥高五 Farewell to Kao Five, My Nephew	
690	赠裴司马 To Commander P'ei	
692	叙旧赠江阳宰陆调 To T'iao Lu, Magistrate of Rivershine, Talking about the Old Days	
696	赠从孙义兴宰铭 To My Grandnephew, Ming Li, Magistrate of Rightrise	

700	草创大还赠柳官迪	
	To Kuanti Liu upon the First Concoction of Gold Pills	
704	赠崔司户文昆季	
	To Wenk'un Ts'ui, a Household Registrar	
707	赠溧阳宋少府陟	
	To Chih Sung, Sheriff of Lishine	
710	戏赠郑溧阳	
	To Cheng, Magistrate of Lishine for Fun	
712	赠僧崖公	
	To Monk Cliff	
716	游溧阳北湖亭望瓦屋山怀古赠同旅	
	To My Vagrant Partner at the Kiosk North of Lishine Lake While Taking a View of Mt. Tiles	
719	醉后赠从甥高镇	
	To Chen Kao, My Nephew, When I'm Drunk	
721	赠秋浦柳少府	
	To Liu, a County Sheriff of Autumn Shore	
723	赠崔秋浦三首	
	To Ts'ui, Magistrate of Autumn Shore, Three Poems	
728	望九华赠青阳韦仲堪	
	To Chungk'an Wei, Magistrate of Blueshine While Looking at Mt. Nine Flowers	

古近体诗五十三首
Old-new Rhythmic Poetry, 53 Poems

秋浦歌十七首

A Song of Autumn Shore, 17 Poems

其 一

秋浦长似秋，
萧条使人愁。
客愁不可度，
行上东大楼。
正西望长安，
下见江水流。
寄言向江水，
汝意忆侬不。
遥传一掬泪，
为我达扬州。

No. 1

Autumn Shore's long in autumn hues；
Its bleakness fills me up with woes.
My sadness is beyond measure；
I go to East Tower for pleasure.
Atop，Long Peace I gaze upon；
Below，the River does flow on.
I ask the River flowing free：
Do you haply remember me?
Please pass a handful of my tear
To Yangchow，to my compeers dear.

* Autumn Shore: southwest of today's Kuich'ih County, Poolton (Ch'ihchow), Anhui Province, rich in silver and copper resources.
* Long Peace: Ch'ang'an if transliterated, the capital of the T'ang Empire, with 1,000,000 inhabitants, the largest walled city ever built by man, and a cosmopolis of world religions: Buddhism, Confucianism, Wordism, Nestorianism, Zoroastrianism, and even Islamism represented by Saracens. It was the wonder of the age that reached the pinnacle of brilliance in Emperor Deepsire's reign: The main castle with its nine-fold gates, the thirty-six imperial palaces, pillars of gold, innumerable mansions and villas of noblemen, the broad avenues thronged with motley crowds of townsfolk, gallants on horseback, and mandarin cars drawn by yokes of black oxen, countless houses of pleasure, which opened their doors by night all made this city a kaleidoscope of miracles.
* Yangchow: an important city in today's Chiangsu Province, the greatest port in China and the centre of luxury trades in the T'ang dynasty.

其 二

秋浦猿夜愁，
黄山堪白头。
清溪非陇水，
翻作断肠流。
欲去不得去，
薄游成久游。
何年是归日，
雨泪下孤舟。

No. 2

The river hears apes shrill at night;
The mountain sees its own hair white.
The creek does not the brook succeed,
But like it flows along to bleed.
I would like to run but can't run;
A short tour becomes a long one.
Which year, which day can I home go?
To the lonely boat my tears flow!

* apes: a large, tailless primate, as a gorilla or chimpanzee, loosely any monkey, often referring to monkeys in Pai Li's poems.

其 三

秋浦锦驼鸟，
人间天上稀。
山鸡羞渌水，
不敢照毛衣。

No. 3

The river sees an ostrich fair;
Between Heaven and earth it's rare.
A pheasant dare not show its plume,
Though it's beautiful like a bloom.

* ostrich: a large camel-like swift-running bird with beautiful plumage, usually a bird of the desert. It is the largest and most powerful bird, and has a long neck, very long legs with two toes on each foot, and small useless wings. The white tail and wing feathers of the mail are used in millinery and as brimming.
* pheasant: a long-tailed gallinaceous bird noted for the gorgeous plumage of the male.

其 四

两鬓入秋浦，
一朝飒已衰。
猿声催白发，
长短尽成丝。

No. 4

In Autumn Shore I stand ashore,
The morning sees me age, age more.
Apes' shrills urge my hair to grow gray,
So tasseled that the hairlines sway.

* Autumn Shore: southwest of today's Kuich'ih County, Anhui Province, rich in silver and copper resources.

其 五

秋浦多白猿，
超腾若飞雪。
牵引条上儿，
饮弄水中月。

No. 5

Autumn Shore teems with monkeys white,
Jumping, leaping like snow in flight.
On the twigs their children they tow
To play a drink of moonlit flow.

* monkeys white: white monkeys or monkeys growing white hair.

其 六

愁作秋浦客,
强看秋浦花。
山川如剡县,
风日似长沙。

No. 6

In Autumn Shore I feel in gloom;
I force myself to see plants bloom.
Autumn Shore's like Shan's hills or rills;
Its landscape, like Longsand's, all thrills.

* Shan: a county in today's Chechiang Province.
* Longsand: Long Sand, Changsha if transliterated, the capital city of present-day Hunan Province.

其 七

醉上山公马，
寒歌宁戚牛。
空吟白石烂，
泪满黑貂裘。

No. 7

So drunk, on Hillman's horse I ride;
And I sing with Ning's ox beside.
The White Stone Breaks I sing in vain;
With tears my marten black I stain.

* Hillman: referring to the fifth son of T'ao Shan (one of the Seven Sages of the Bamboo Grove in the Chin dynasty). He was gentle and graceful as his father. When he was an official, the nation was falling apart and other officials were worried and depressed. Hillman, however, lived a casual life. Every time he hanged out, he would hold a banquet and often got drunk at the High Sun Pool.
* Ning: Ch'i Ning in full name, a meritorious statesman of Ch'i in the Spring and Autumn period. In his early age, Ning was poor and had no access to officialdom. When Lord Collumn of Ch'i was passing by, Ning knocked on an ox horn and sang out his frustration and attracted attention eventually.
* ox: any of several bovid ruminants as cattle, buffaloes, bison, gaur, and yaks; especially a domesticated bull (Bos taurus), used as a draft animal, a symbol of diligence in Chinese culture.
* *The White Stone Breaks*: a song that Ning sang.
* marten: a weasel-like fur-bearing carnivorous animal (genus *Martes*) having arboreal habits as the pine marten and the large sturdy fisher marten; also the fur of a marten used for the making of expensive clothing.

其 八

秋浦千重岭，
水车岭最奇。
天倾欲堕石，
水拂寄生枝。

No. 8

Autumn Shore has hills upon hills,
Of which Waterwheel gives all thrills.
The sky seems to fall down with stone;
The twigs stir the stream as if blown.

* Autumn Shore: a county of T'ang, 40 kilometers southwest of Poolton in today's Anhui Province, a scenic place teeming with flora and fauna and rich in silver and copper resources.
* Waterwheel: a peak in today's Poolton (Ch'ihchow), Anhui Province.

其 九

江祖一片石，
青天扫画屏。
题诗留万古，
绿字锦苔生。

No. 9

The rock called Riverstone towers high,
Like a screen scraping the blue sky.
The inscriptions last long with gloss;
The characters are green with moss.

* Riverstone: 12.5 kilometers from Poolton in today's Anhui Province, a rock thrusting out of water dozens of meters tall, called Riverstone or Mt. Riverstone.
* screen: a curtain which separates or cuts off, shelters or protects as a light partition, a common image in Chinese literature. A poem in *The Book of Songs* reads like this:"You wait for me before the screen; / Your hat-rings white do tinkle clean, / And your rubies brilliantly sheen."
* moss: a tiny, delicate green bryophytic plant growing on damp decaying wood, wet ground, humid rocks or trees, producing capsules which open by an operculum and contain spores. Under a poet's writing brush, this tiny, insignificant plant may arouse a poetic feeling or imagination, as was written by Mei Yüan, a poet in the Ching dynasty:"Where the sun does not arrive, / Springtime does on its own thrive. / The moss flowers like rice tiny, / Rush to bloom like the peony."

其 十

千千石楠树，
万万女贞林。
山山白鹭满，
涧涧白猿吟。
君莫向秋浦，
猿声碎客心。

No. 10

So many moor besoms there stand;
The woods of privets there expand.
White egrets fly across the hills;
White monkeys shrill over the rills.
To Autumn Shore don't you depart;
The monkey's cries will break your heart.

* moor besom: an evergreen plant or shrub, photinia serrulata in Latin, having young red leaves that turn green as they grow and dense small white flowers.
* privet: an ornamental bushy shrub with white flowers and black berries, used for hedges.
* egret: a heron characterized, in the breeding season, by long and loose plumes drooping over the tail, usually white plumage.
* Autumn Shore: southwest of today's Kuich'ih County, Anhui Province, rich in silver and copper resources.

其十一

逻人横鸟道，
江祖出鱼梁。
水急客舟疾，
山花拂面香。

No. 11

Patrolpass is for birds to pass;
Riverstone sees weirs towing grass.
The water fast hastens the boats;
To my face the mountain's balm floats.

* Riverstone: a big stone in a river. 12.5 kilometers from Poolton in today's Anhui Province, there is a big rock thrusting out of water dozens of meters tall, called Riverstone or Mt. Riverstone.

其十二

水如一匹练，
此地即平天。
耐可乘明月，
看花上酒船。

No. 12

The water is like silk cloth white;
With the sky it has the same height.
Come, to the moon we can climb up;
Let's view blossoms and drink a cup.

* The water is like silk cloth white: the moonlit water is white e'en at night, and seems to be near the sky, so the poet says one can climb up to the moon.
* the moon: the celestial body that revolves around the earth from west to east as a satellite, which appears at night and gives off shining silvery light, an image of purity and solitude in Chinese culture.

其十三

渌水净素月，
月明白鹭飞。
郎听采菱女，
一道夜歌归。

No. 13

The pool does the moon purify;
The moon bright, the white egrets fly.
The lad listens to the maid croon,
And they go back home with the moon.

* egret: a heron characterized, in the breeding season, by long and loose plumes drooping over the tail, usually white plumage.
* The lad listens to the maid croon: It's a custom in Wu and Ch'u to sing while gathering water chestnuts or lotus pods.
* the moon: the planet of the earth, which appears at night and gives off shining silvery light, an image of purity and solitude in Chinese culture.

其十四

炉火照天地，
红星乱紫烟。
赧郎明月夜，
歌曲动寒川。

No. 14

The forge lights up the earth and sky;
The sparks scatter the smoke on high.
The moonlit blacksmith, o behold,
With his song moves the river cold.

* forge: an open fireplace for heating metal to be hammered. As Autumn Shore is rich in silver and copper, forging is popular there.

其十五

白发三千丈，
缘愁似个长。
不知明镜里，
何处得秋霜。

No. 15

My gray hair grows three miles long;
As long as my cares there hung.
From where on earth, I feel lost,
Does the mirror get the frost?

* My gray hair grows three miles long: a hyperbole that suits the great poet's great mind.

其十六

秋浦田舍翁，
采鱼水中宿。
妻子张白鹇，
结罝映深竹。

No. 16

In Autumn Shore the farmer moors;
For night fishing his boat he oars.
His wife to entrap pheasants white
In the bamboo sets a net tight.

* Autumn Shore: the place in today's Anhui that was once rich in mineral resources and animals.
* pheasant: a long-tailed gallinaceous bird noted for the gorgeous plumage of the male.

其十七

桃波一步地，
了了语声闻。
黯与山僧别，
低头礼白云。

No. 17

Peach Slope is not far off from here;
The folks' talk one can clearly hear.
To the monk I say adieu now,
And to the floating clouds I bow.

* Peach Slope: a slope with a pool below called Jade Mirror.

当涂赵炎少府粉图山水歌

峨眉高出西极天,
罗浮直与南溟连。
名公绎思挥彩笔,
驱山走海置眼前。
满堂空翠如可扫,
赤城霞气苍梧烟。
洞庭潇湘意渺绵,
三江七泽情洄沿。
惊涛汹涌向何处,
孤舟一去迷归年。
征帆不动亦不旋,
飘如随风落天边。
心摇目断兴难尽,
几时可到三山巅。
西峰峥嵘喷流泉,
横石蹙水波潺湲。
东崖合沓蔽轻雾,
深林杂树空芊绵。
此中冥昧失昼夜,
隐几寂听无鸣蝉。
长松之下列羽客,
对坐不语南昌仙。
南昌仙人赵夫子,
妙年历落青云士。
讼庭无事罗众宾,
杳然如在丹青里。
五色粉图安足珍,

真仙可以全吾身。
若待功成拂衣去,
武陵桃花笑杀人。

Viewing a Painting at Tangt'u, in the House of Yan Chao, a Constable

Mt. Brow's high, exceeding the western sky;
The La Phu Mountains with South Sea there tie.
The painter smart his painting brush now plies
And drives the mountains and seas to my eyes.
A whole houseful of green if one can sweep,
The vapor and mist will from Red Town peep.
Lake Cavehall surges up and the Hsiang flows;
Three rivers and seven swamps make good views.
Where are the waves going, surging away?
The boat once gone won't come back, there astray.
Unmoved seems the sail, not rowed looks the boat,
As if blown by wind, in distance afloat.
My heart sways and my eyes shine without stop;
When will the boat moor at the mountaintop?
The western peaks jut high, cataracts fall;
The boulder laid aside hears the stream call.
The eastern cliffs are veiled by thinning fog;
The deep forest stretches to the lush bog.
No night or day one can discern, so still;
Sitting at desk, I hear no locusts trill.
A few hermits sit under the pine trees,
Plum Foo, the immortal, at silent ease.
The immortal's from Southboom, Chao by name;

In full prime and upright, he wins good fame.
No disputes, he invites guests to good wine,
A picture of hermits, all souls divine.
Though this painting is so vivid and good,
To be a real saint in real scenes I would.
Upon success I'll wave my sleeve and go;
The peach flowers in Fairyland with balm blow!

* Yan Chao: a friend of Pai Li's.
* Mt. Brow: Mt. Omei if transliterated, a famous mountain located in present-day Ssuch'uan Province.
* the La Phu Mountains: mountains in present-day Kuangtung Province where Ko Hung, a hermit in the Chin dynasty, used to live in seclusion.
* South Sea: what is South China Sea today.
* Red Town: a mountain in present-day Chechiang Province.
* Lake Cavehall: a lake in modern-day Hunan Province, with an area of 3,879.2 square kilometers and 803.2 kilometers in circumference.
* locust: any of a family of widely distributed orthopterous insects having short antennae, especially those of migratory habits.
* Plum Foo: a constable of Southboom (Nanch'ang) in the Han dynasty, who was said to have become immortal.
* Southboom: Nanch'ang if transliterated, the capital of today's Chianghsi Province, a city first built in 202 B.C., having an important position of military and economy in Chinese history.
* peach: any tree of the genus *Prunus Percica*, blooming brilliantly and bearing fruit, a fleshy, juicy, edible drupe, considered sacred in China, a symbol of romance, prosperity and longevity.
* Fairyland: an ideal abode for immortals, sometimes thought of as being in the middle of East Sea, sometimes in the sky.

永王东巡歌十一首
Prince E'er on East March, 11 Poems

其 一

永王正月东出师，
天子遥分龙虎旗。
楼船一举风波静，
江汉翻为燕鹜池。

No. 1

The first moon Prince E'er on march will east go;
At the Crown's order, banners and flags flow.
The tower ships fall silent, all waves fall still;
The torrents hushed, Swallow Pool's a calm fill.

* Prince E'er: Lin Li (? - A.D. 757), the 16th son of Emperor Deepsire of T'ang, brilliant and capable, assigned to guard the south during Lushan An's Rebellion.
* Swallow Pool: a pool about two kilometers in circumference, which was dug by Wu Liu (? - 144 B.C.), King Piety of Liang in the Han dynasty.

其 二

三川北虏乱如麻,
四海南奔似永嘉。
但用东山谢安石,
为君谈笑净胡沙。

No. 2

To the Three Rivers Hun foes swarm pell-mell;
The folks escape as if from E'erwell Hell.
If General Hsieh is ordered to command,
He will, with a laugh, sweep off the Hun sand.

* the Three Rivers: referring to the drainage area of the three rivers, that is, the Yellow River, the Lo River and the Ee River, approximately Honan Prefecture, i.e. today's Honan Province.
* E'erwell: Yungchia if transliterated, a county in Fuchien Province.
* Hun: one of barbaric nomadic Asian peoples who frequently invaded China, a general term referring to all northern or western invaders.
* General Hsieh: referring to An Hsieh (A.D. 320 – A.D. 385), a general, statesman and renowned scholar in the Eastern Chin dynasty. When Hsieh was playing chess with his friends, a letter arrived but he continued to play without any hint or change of expression after reading it. When a friend asked him about the letter, he answered, quite composed: "My son has won." Not until Hsieh went back to his room did he realize that he was too happy to find his shoes had already broken.

其 三

雷鼓嘈嘈喧武昌，
云旗猎猎过寻阳。
秋毫不犯三吴悦，
春日遥看五色光。

No. 3

The drums thump, thump in Mightboom and it drown;
The flags flutter through Bankshine, the whole town.
Not troubled, so pleased are the people there;
From afar, they look into the spring fair.

* Mightboom: Wuch'ang if transliterated, one of the three towns that make today's Wuhan, Hupei Province.
* Bankshine: a former name of the Nine Rivers (Ch'iuchiang).

其 四

龙盘虎踞帝王州，
帝子金陵访故丘。
春风试暖昭阳殿，
明月还过鸦鹊楼。

No. 4

What an important place, what a king land;
Prince E'er viewing the Gold Hills does here stand.
The spring zephyr warms the Palace of Glare;
On Magpie Tower there hangs the moon so fair.

* the Gold Hills: the mountains in Nanking. An alias of Nanking is Gold Hill, named after the hills.
* Prince E'er: Lin Li (? – A.D. 757), the 16th son of Emperor Deepsire of T'ang, assigned to guard the south during Lushan An's Rebellion.
* Palace of Glare: the palace where an empress dowager dwelt.
* Magpie Tower: a building in Gold Hills.
* the moon: the celestial body that revolves around the earth from west to east as a satellite, which appears at night and gives off shining silvery light, an image of purity and solitude in Chinese culture.

其 五

二帝巡游俱未回，
五陵松柏使人哀。
诸侯不救河南地，
更喜贤王远道来。

No. 5

The two Lords have not come back from their cruise;
The pines on the Five Hills bring people rues.
No vassal lords come to rescue South Land;
The sage prince has come to offer his hand.

* two Lords: referring to Emperor Deepsire and his successor. The line is a euphemism for the fact that Emperor Deepsire escaped to Shu, present-day Ssuch'uan during Lushan An's Rebellion.
* Five Hills: referring to the tombs of five former emperors.

其 六

丹阳北固是吴关,
画出楼台云水间。
千岩烽火连沧海,
两岸旌旗绕碧山。

No. 6

Mt. North Firm was once the Wu Pass of yore;
The tower looms between the sky and the shore.
The fire of war does stretch to the ocean;
The flags on the banks wave to the mountain.

* Mt. North Firm: on the east part of Chenchiang near the Long River, 53 meters high.

其 七

王出三江按五湖，
楼船跨海次扬都。
战舰森森罗虎士，
征帆一一引龙驹。

No. 7

Three Rivers and Five Lakes see Prince E'er's men;
His warships from the sea reach Yangchow then.
The fighters aboard do strike one with awe;
The tower ships send war horses to the war.

* Three Rivers and Five Lakes: referring to the three rivers and lakes within the reach of Lake Grand (Taihu).
* Prince E'er: Lin Li (? - A.D. 757), the 16th son of Emperor Deepsire of T'ang, assigned to garrison South Land during Lushan An's Rebellion.
* Yangchow: a city in today's Chiangsu Province and an important port city in the T'ang dynasty.

其 八

长风挂席势难回，
海动山倾古月摧。
君看帝子浮江日，
何似龙骧出峡来。

No. 8

The wind blows the sails forward, no retreat;
The mountains like armies would Huns defeat.
Prince E'er would cross the river now to fight,
Like General Dragon marched east with might.

* Hun: one of barbaric nomadic Asian peoples who frequently invaded China, a general term referring to all northern or western invaders.
* Prince E'er: Lin Li (? – A.D. 757), the 16th son of Emperor Deepsire of T'ang, assigned to guard the south during Lushan An's Rebellion.
* General Dragon: a declared title of ancient generals.

其 九

祖龙浮海不成桥，
汉武寻阳空射蛟。
我王楼舰轻秦汉，
却似文皇欲渡辽。

No. 9

An ocean bridge Sire Dragon failed to make;
In Bankshine Lord Martial shot but missed Snake.
Our warships could Ch'in and Han's might ignore,
Like King Civil crossing the sea to Liao.

* Sire Dragon: referring to Emperor First of Ch'in (259 B.C.- 210 B.C.), who established the first unified empire of China. As legend goes, when Emperor First was building a stone bridge over the ocean, Sea God was under water, helping to erect piers. Emperor First asked to give him audience, but Sea God excused himself, saying that he was too ugly to show up. Emperor First dived to see him, but Sea God disappeared with anger. The emperor hardly managed to shore and the unfinished bridge collapsed.
* Lord Martial: Emperor Martial of Han (156 B.C.- 87 B.C.), the seventh emperor of the Han dynasty, a prominent statesman, strategist and poet, who made his empire prosperous in all aspects.
* Ch'in and Han's might: a metaphor for great military power.
* King Civil: King Civil of Chough (1152 B.C.- 1056 B.C.), the founder of Chough, a wise king in history.
* Liao: the drainage area of the Liao River, mainly today's Liaoning Province.

其 十

帝宠贤王入楚关，
扫清江汉始应还。
初从云梦开朱邸，
更取金陵作小山。

No. 10

His Majesty sent Prince E'er to guard Ch'u;
He should come back once he swept Rivers Two.
In Cloud-and-Dream a red mansion he'd build;
And he'd move the Gold Hills there as a shield.

* Prince E'er: Lin Li (cir. A.D. 721 - A.D. 757), the 16th son of Emperor Deepsire of T'ang, assigned to guard the south during Lushan An's Rebellion.
* Ch'u: a metonymy for South Land.
* Rivers Two: the Han River and the Long River, referring to South Land.
* Cloud-and-Dream: referring to the lake area in today's Hupei Province.
* the Gold Hills: what is today's the Rosegold Hills, in today's Nanking, whose alias is Gold Hill.

其十一

试借君王玉马鞭，
指挥戎虏坐琼筵。
南风一扫胡尘静，
西入长安到日边。

No. 11

May I borrow your Lord-granted-whip once
That I'll wave at a feast to expel Huns?
With a blow of wind I would wipe them all,
And come back with glee to the capital.

* Huns: nomadic barbarians north and west of China, which frequently invaded China, who had no trade but battle and carnage, no fields or plough lands but only wastes where white bones lay scattered over yellow sands.

上皇西巡南京歌十首

His Majesty's Tour West to the Southern Town, Ten Poems

其 一

胡尘轻拂建章台，
圣主西巡蜀道来。
剑壁门高五千尺，
石为楼阁九天开。

No. 1

The Hun dust over the palace does sway;
His Majesty comes west to the Shu Way.
Sword Gate juts, reaching five thousand feet high;
The crag like a tower holds up the Ninth Sky.

* Hun: one of barbaric nomadic Asian peoples who frequently invaded China, a general term referring to all northern or western invaders.
* Shu: a former name for Ssuch'uan, one of the earliest kingdoms in China, founded by Silkworm according to legend. In the Three Kingdoms period, a new Shu was established by Pei Liu, hence one of the three kingdoms in that period.
* Sword Gate: Sword Gate Pass: a strategic pass with a plank road built along cliffs by Bright Chuke in the Three Kingdoms period, in present-day Ssuch'uan Province.
* the Ninth Sky: the empyrean, the highest of Heavens, the highest of the nine layers of the sky according to Chinese legend.

其 二

九天开出一成都,
万户千门入画图。
草树云山如锦绣,
秦川得及此间无。

No. 2

The Ninth Sky reveals Silkton, the Shu town,
Thousands of households like a picture drawn.
Grass, trees, clouds and hills make a brocade rare;
Can the capital with this town compare?

* the Ninth Sky: the empyrean, the highest of Heavens, the highest of the nine layers of the sky according to Chinese legend, and a similar notion in Dante's *Divina Commedia* in the west, *The Lüs' Spring and Autumn* in China and Buddhist Sutras from India.
* Silkton: the capital of Shu, where the Silk River runs through.

其 三

华阳春树号新丰，
行入新都若旧宫。
柳色未饶秦地绿，
花光不减上阳红。

No. 3

Flowershine as Newrich is live with spring trees;
New Town like the old palace does Lord please.
The willows do the green of Ch'in outshine;
The blooms here surpass Uppershine's blooms fine.

* Flowershine: a reigning title of Shu, here referring to Ch'engtu.
* Newrich: a county, located in the northeast of Lintung, celebrated for fine wine.
* Ch'in: the Ch'in State or the State of Ch'in (905 B.C - 206 B.C.), one of the most powerful vassal states in the Chough dynasty, which developed into the first unified regime of China, i.e. the Ch'in Empire.
* Uppershine: a royal palace built in Loshine.

其　四

谁道君王行路难，
六龙西幸万人欢。
地转锦江成渭水，
天回玉垒作长安。

No. 4

Who says an emperor goes a hard way?
His six-horse cart going west makes one gay.
The earth sees the Silk like the Wei flow on;
Heaven makes Mt. Jade the capital town.

* the Silk: the Silk River, a branch from the upper reach of the Yangtze River. As legend goes, a pious lady who washed in the river the filthy robe of a Buddhist monk who fell into a dunghill. No sooner had she dipped the robe into the water than the river filled with bright flowers, which is said to be the origin of the industry of making lovely silk brocades.
* the Wei: the Wei River: the largest branch of the Yellow River, originating from today's Mt. Birdmouse in Kansu Province, flowing through Precious Rooster, Allshine, Long Peace, and meeting the Yellow River at T'ung Pass.
* Mt. Jade: in today's Capital River Weir (Tuchiangyan), Ssuch'uan Province.

其 五

万国同风共一时，
锦江何谢曲江池。
石镜更明天上月，
后宫亲得照蛾眉。

No. 5

All the land rolls on at the zephyr's call;
Is the Bent better than the Silk at all?
Stone Mirror does outshine the moon so fair;
Court ladies look into it to do hair.

* the Bent: Ch'uchiang if transliterated, a royal park of T'ang, located in the southeast of Long Peace, the capital.
* the Silk: the Silk River, Chinchiang if transliterated, the upper reach of the Yangtze River.
* Stone Mirror: referring to a tomb in Shu. According to historical records, a king of Shu married a charming mountain spirit and built her a tomb after her death. As is said, there was a stone mirror hanging above.
* the moon: the celestial body that revolves around the earth from west to east as a satellite, which appears at night and gives off shining silvery light, an image of purity and solitude in Chinese culture.

其 六

濯锦清江万里流，
云帆龙舸下扬州。
北地虽夸上林苑，
南京还有散花楼。

No. 6

The Silk River does ten thousand miles flow;
The dragon boats set their sails to Yangchow.
The north land boasts the Royal Park to show;
The south town has a tower with flowers to throw.

* the Silk River: the Silk, a river across Silkton, present-day Ch'engtu.
* Yangchow: an important city in today's Chiangsu Province, the greatest port in China and the centre of luxury trades in the T'ang dynasty.
* the Royal Park: a metaphor used in this poem, referring to High Park, an imperial park that Lord Martial of Han built on the site of a discarded park of Ch'in.

其 七

锦水东流绕锦城，
星桥北挂象天星。
四海此中朝圣主，
峨眉山下列仙庭。

No. 7

The Silk flows around Silkton, the Shu town;
The seven bridges are just like the Plough.
All the world come here to worship the crown;
Divine courts are deployed beside Mt. Brow.

* the Silk: the Silk River, Chinchiang if transliterated, the upper reach of the Yangtze River.
* Silkton: alias Ch'engtu, a city prosperous with fine silk.
* the Plough: the group of seven stars commonly called Charles's Wain or the Dipper, sometimes also Ursa Major.
* Mt. Brow: Mt. Omei if transliterated, a famous mountain located in Shu, present-day Ssuch'uan.

其 八

秦开蜀道置金牛，
汉水元通星汉流。
天子一行遗圣迹，
锦城长作帝王州。

No. 8

Ch'in cast a gold bull for a pass to Shu,
The path's like the Han flowing to the blue.
His Majesty to west left trails divine;
Silkton's since turned into Emperor's Sign.

* Ch'in: the Ch'in State or the State of Ch'in (905 B.C.- 206 B.C.), one of the most powerful vassal states in the Chough dynasty, which developed into the first unified regime of China, i.e., the Ch'in Empire.
* a gold bull: referring to Gold Bull Artery to Shu. Lord Letter of Ch'in (356 B.C.- 311 B.C.) wanted to suppress Shu, but there was no access. Knowing Shu's king was greedy, Lord Letter of Ch'in then made a fake gold bull and gave it to Shu as a present. The King of Shu was pleased and built an artery to receive the gold bull. Having the artery, Ch'in successfully took over Shu.
* Shu: one of the earliest kingdoms in China, founded by Silkworm according to legend. In the Three Kingdoms period, a new Shu was established by Pei Liu, hence one of the three kingdoms in that period.
* the Han: the Han River, the longest branch of the Long River, having an important position in Chinese history.
* Silkton: today's Ch'engtu, the capital of Ssuch'uan Province.

其 九

水绿天青不起尘,
风光和暖胜三秦。
万国烟花随玉辇,
西来添作锦江春。

No. 9

The stream green, the sky blue, no flying sand;
It is warmer and better than Ch'in's land.
The mist and blooms follow his sedan cart;
To bedeck the Silk all would do their part.

* Ch'in: the Ch'in State or the State of Ch'in (905 B.C – 206 B.C.), one of the most powerful vassal states in the Chough dynasty, which developed into the first unified regime of China, i.e., the Ch'in Empire.
* the Silk: the Silk River, Chinchiang if transliterated, the upper reach of the Yangtze River.

其 十

剑阁重关蜀北门，
上皇归马若云屯。
少帝长安开紫极，
双悬日月照乾坤。

No. 10

The Sword Pavilion guards Shu's northern gate;
His Majesty's carts roll like clouds, how great!
In Long Peace, the Lord welcomes Upper Lord,
The glare of the two suns is to all poured.

* Long Peace: Ch'ang'an if transliterated, the metropolis of gold, the capital of the T'ang Empire, with 1,000,000 inhabitants, the largest walled city ever built by man, and now the capital of today's Sha'anhsi Province. Long Peace saw the wonder of Chinese civilization that reached the pinnacle of brilliance in Emperor Deepsire's reign.
* the Lord: Heng Li (A.D. 711 - A.D. 762), Emperor Deepsire's third son, the 7th emperor of T'ang, who was enthroned during Lushan An's Rebellion.
* Sword Pavilion: a strategic pass with a plank road built along cliffs in present-day Ssuch'uan Province.
* Upper Lord: Emperor Deepsire, the 6th emperor of T'ang who gave the throne to his third son, Heng Li, during Lushan An's Rebellion.

峨眉山月歌

峨眉山月半轮秋，
影入平羌江水流。
夜发清溪向三峡，
思君不见下渝州。

A Song of the Moon o'er Mt. Brow

Half a disc of moon over Mt. Brow glows;
Its autumn shadow cast to the Peace flows.
From Clear Creek to Three Gorges I go at night,
Rowing past Yüchow without you in sight.

* the moon: the planet of the earth, which appears at night and gives off shining silvery light, an image of purity and solitude in Chinese culture.
* Mt. Brow: Mt. Omei if transliterated, a famous mountain located in Shu.
* the Peace: Pingch'iang if transliterated, a river located in Shu.
* Three Gorges: referring to the three gorges of the Long River, including Big Pond Gorge, Witch Gorge, and Westridge Gorge, a set of spectacular gorges formed where the Long River cuts its way through the formidable Witch Mountains, forming a three-hundred-kilometer stretch of very narrow canyons.
* Yüchow: a former name of Ch'ungch'ing.

峨眉山月歌送蜀僧晏入中京

我在巴东三峡时,
西看明月忆峨眉。
月出峨眉照沧海,
与人万里长相随。
黄鹤楼前月华白,
此中忽见峨眉客。
峨眉山月还送君,
风吹西到长安陌。
长安大道横九天,
峨眉山月照秦川。
黄金狮子乘高座,
白玉麈尾谈重玄。
我似浮云殢吴越,
君逢圣主游丹阙。
一振高名满帝都,
归时还弄峨眉月。

A Song of the Moon o'er Mt. Brow to Yan, a Monk from Shu, Who Comes to Capital

When I live at Three Gorges, in East Pa there,
I look west to Mt. Brow for the moon fair.
The moon over Mt. Brow shines to the sea
And will for ten thousand miles follow me.
Yellow Crane Tower upholds the moon so fair;
From Mt. Brow you suddenly appear there.

The moon over Mt. Brow will follow you
West to Long Peace while wind rises to blow.
To the Ninth Sky rolls on the Long Peace Way;
Luna from Mt. Brow to Ch'in's plains sheds ray.
With golden lions, sitting on a high mound,
You talk the profoundest of the profound.
While I wander like a cloud in South Land,
You with His Majesty tour altars grand.
When you have enjoyed fame and grace enow,
Pray come back to the moon atop Mt. Brow.

* Three Gorges: referring to the three gorges of the Long River, including Big Pond Gorge, Witch Gorge, and Westridge Gorge. It implies the area around the three gorges.
* Yellow Crane Tower: a famous tower built by Wu in A.D. 223, located on the top of Mt. Snake, overlooking the Long River, one of the three historical attractions (the other two being Shine River Pavillion and the Old Lute Platform) of today's Wuhan, Hupei Province.
* Long Peace: Ch'ang'an if transliterated, a capital of sixteen dynasties in Chinese history. When the T'ang Empire adopted it as its capital, it reached its fullest glory as a cosmopolis with 1,000,000 inhabitants, the largest walled city ever built by man. It is now the capital of Sha'anhsi Province, the starting point of the New Silk Road.
* the Ninth Sky: the high sky, the vast empyrean, the highest of the nine layers of the sky according to Chinese legend.
* Ch'in's plain: referring to the plain in the reach of the River Wei where the ancient capital Long Peace was located.
* lion: a large, yellowish-brown or tawny feline carnivorous mammal, a symbol of courage or a metaphor for a man of leonine character or mien.

赤壁歌送别

二龙争战决雌雄，
赤壁楼船扫地空。
烈火张天照云海，
周瑜于此破曹公。
君去沧江望澄碧，
鲸鲵唐突留馀迹。
一一书来报故人，
我欲因之壮心魄。

Farewell at Red Wall

Two dragons fought hard, a winner to be,
Warships at Red Wall, like towers on the sea.
The fire lit up the earth and sky, ablaze;
In this war, Yü Chou would Ts'ao Ts'ao erase.
Now to the broad sea you're going to sail,
To ruins left by Salamander and Whale.
To tell what you've seen, you can write to me,
So that inspired and high raised I can be.

* dragon: a fabulous serpent-like giant winged animal, a totem of the Chinese nation, a symbol of benevolence and sovereignty in Chinese culture.
* two dragons: referring to Ts'ao Ts'ao (A.D. 155 – A.D. 220) and Ch'üan Sun (A.D. 182 – A.D. 252), two military powers in the Three Kingdoms period.
* Red Wall: In the year of 208, Ch'üan Sun and Pei Liu fought against Ts'ao Ts'ao at Red Wall. Ch'üan Sun's general, Yü Chou, burnt Ts'ao's army by feigning surrender.
* Yü Chou: Yü Chou (A.D. 175 – A.D. 210), a famous general in the late Eastern Han

dynasty or the Three Kingdoms period.
* Salamander and Whale: referring to Ts'ao's unjust army. The salamander, a tailed lizard-like amphibian, once popularly believed to be able to live in fire, and the whale, a giant sea mammal, together are used as a metaphor for threatening invaders or rebels.

江 夏 行

忆昔娇小姿，
春心亦自持。
为言嫁夫婿，
得免长相思。
谁知嫁商贾，
令人却愁苦。
自从为夫妻，
何曾在乡土？
去年下扬州，
相送黄鹤楼。
眼看帆去远，
心逐江水流，
只言期一载，
谁谓历三秋。
使妾肠欲断，
恨君情悠悠。
东家西舍同时发，
北去南来不逾月。
未知行李游何方，
作个音书能断绝。
适来往南浦，
欲问西江船。
正见当垆女，
红妆二八年。
一种为人妻，
独自多悲凄。
对镜便垂泪，

逢人只欲啼。
不如轻薄儿，
旦暮长追随。
悔作商人妇，
青春长别离。
如今正好同欢乐，
君去容华谁得知？

In Riversummer

When I was a girl, I recall,
I could control myself for all.
Then I was urged to go marry
Lest in lovesickness I tarry.
I married a merchant, who knows?
Each day I suffered many woes.
Since the day I became your wife,
Have you e'er cared about my life?
You did go to Yangchow last year;
Yellow Crane saw you disappear.
While I saw your sail far off go,
My heart with the waves did flow.
You said in one year you'd be back;
It has been three years now, alack.
I am filled up with sadness blue,
Hating you like the endless flow.
Our neighbors east and west left the same day;
Less than a month they came back home to stay.
Where on earth are you touring? I don't know.
I'd write a letter. There's no postman, no!

So I come along to South Shore,

Asking: Any boat comes to moor?

Here I see a sixteen, clad fine,

Who's a young woman selling wine.

We are both wives, both fully grown,

Why am I, so sad, left alone?

At the mirror I sadly sigh,

And when seeing people I cry.

I'd rather I'd married a fop,

Following him, to go or stop.

A merchant's wife I am, sad, smart;

In prime, for long we are apart.

By now we should have enjoyed our best while;

But you are gone, who knows my frown or smile?

* Riversummer: an ancient town tracing back to 350 B.C. when Sha-e was established and was officially renamed Riversummer in A.D. 589, one of the three towns that constitutes Wuhan, now called Chianghsia District under Wuhan.
* Yangchow: a city in today's Chiangsu Province and an important port city in the T'ang dynasty.
* Yellow Crane: referring to Yellow Crane Tower built in the Three Kingdoms period, one of the most famous ancient towers in China, in present-day Wuhan, Hupei.

怀 仙 歌

一鹤东飞过沧海，
放心散漫知何在。
仙人浩歌望我来，
应攀玉树长相待。
尧舜之事不足惊，
自馀嚣嚣直可轻。
巨鳌莫载三山去，
我欲蓬莱顶上行。

A Song of Immortals

A crane flies to the east, to the blue sea;
Where can I rest my heart, where can it be?
The immortals sing and expect me now;
They're waiting for me, leaning on a bough.
Mound and Hibiscus, so trivial, both fail,
Having left in this world only their tale.
Giant Turtle, don't carry the isles away;
I will climb to the zenith and there stay.

* crane: one of a family of large, long-necked, long-legged, heronlike birds allied to the rails, a symbol of integrity and longevity in Chinese culture, only second to the phoenix in cultural importance.
* Mound and Hibiscus: two legendary sage kings in ancient China.
* Giant Turtle: In Chinese myths, there was a giant turtle carrying the three fairy isles in East Sea.
* zenith: the point directly overhead in the sky or on the celestial sphere, opposed to the nadir.

玉真仙人词

玉真之仙人，
时往太华峰。
清晨鸣天鼓，
飙欻腾双龙。
弄电不辍手，
行云本无踪。
几时入少室，
王母应相逢。

A Lyric for Princess Jade

Real goddess, our Princess, she oft
Climbs Mt. Flora and stays aloft.
At dawn a drum vibrates the skies;
The two dragons o'er her head rise.
She gathers spirit from the space,
And goes like a cloud with no trace.
When on Mt. Smallroom will she rest?
There she can meet with Mother West.

* Princess Jade: Princess Jade (A.D. 692 – A.D. 762), a princess and Wordist in the T'ang dynasty, Pai Li's lover.
* Mt. Flora: one of the Five Sacred Mountains in China, representing the west, regarded as the steepest and saintly mountain in China as it is one of the progenitors of Chinese culture, the shrine of Wordism and the abode of God of Mt. Flora, located in today's Flowershade, Sha'anhsi Province.
* dragon: a fabulous serpent-like giant winged animal that can change its girth and

length, a totem of the Chinese nation, a symbol of benevolence and sovereignty in Chinese culture.

* Mt. Smallroom: one of the mountains that make Mt. Tower, located in present-day Honan Province.
* Mother West: a sovereign goddess living on Mt. Queen in Chinese myths. Her appearance was originally described as human-bodied, tiger-toothed, leopard-tailed and hoopoe-haired. Mother West is regarded as a goddess in charge of women protection, marriage and procreation, and longevity.

清 溪 行

清溪清我心，
水色异诸水。
借问新安江，
见底何如此。
人行明镜中，
鸟度屏风里。
向晚猩猩啼，
空悲远游子。

A Clean Brook

The clean brook can my heart well clean;
From others it's a different sheen.
May I ask the New Peace o'er there?
Can you be the same, just as clear?
It seems through a mirror one goes;
It seems on a screen a bird coos.
As dusk falls, orangutans cry;
A stray vagrant, I sadly sigh.

* the New Peace: the River Hsin'an if transliterated, the New Peace River springing from Mt. Yellow.
* screen: a curtain which separates or cuts off, shelters or protects as a light partition, a common image in Chinese literature. Two lines from a Sung lyric by Haowen Yüan reads like this:"The drizzle falls before my tower's sill; / 'Broidered with crabapples, the screen's chill."
* orangutan: a large anthropoid ape (genus *Pongo* or *Simia*), having brown-reddish hair, brown skin, small ears, doglike teeth, narrow lips, and long arms reaching to the ankles.

酬殷明佐见赠五云裘歌

我吟谢朓诗上语,
朔风飒飒吹飞雨。
谢朓已没青山空,
后来继之有殷公。
粉图珍裘五云色,
晔如晴天散彩虹。
文章彪炳光陆离,
应是素娥玉女之所为。
轻如松花落金粉,
浓似苔锦含碧滋。
远山积翠横海岛,
残霞飞丹映江草。
凝毫采掇花露容,
几年功成夺天造。
故人赠我我不违,
著令山水含清晖。
顿惊谢康乐,
诗兴生我衣。
襟前林壑敛暝色,
袖上云霞收夕霏。
群仙长叹惊此物,
千崖万岭相萦郁。
身骑白鹿行飘飖,
手翳紫芝笑披拂。
相如不足夸鹔鹴,
王恭鹤氅安可方。
瑶台雪花数千点,

片片吹落春风香。
为君持此凌苍苍,
上朝三十六玉皇。
下窥夫子不可及,
矫首相思空断肠。

Thanks to Mingts'o Yin for His Gift of Five Cloud Fur

I croon T'iao Hsieh's verse and like its sad strain,
Like a northern wind, sough, sough thru a rain.
T'iao Hsieh is gone and the mountains are void;
Mister Yin comes instead, as if deployed.
On his clothes patterns and five colors vie,
Like a rainbow beaming under the sky.
The hues seem to be glaring up and down;
That must be Jade Maid's brocade, that must be her gown.
It's so light like gold powder from pine trees;
It's so thick like green moss, a dewy squeeze.
The hills afar green the isles in the sea;
The rainbow east adorns the river lea.
The pistils from the dewy leaves appear;
This piece must have taken many a year.
Your clothes given to me I can't refuse,
Which I will wear to stir up mountain hues.
If Hsieh the great poet sees this gown,
He'll write a poem, to a spurt drawn.
The front is a picture of wooded dale;
The sleeves show dusk clouds that in mist prevail.
At this, fairies are taken to surprise,

On which, peaks and cliffs highly rise.
Wearing it, riding a deer, I'll go miles,
Holding glossy ganoderma, all smiles.
Before it, Ssuma's plumage has no glare;
With it Kung Wang's crane cloak cannot compare.
The Heaven Pool sees countless flakes of snow
That thru balmy air a spring wind does blow.
Wearing it, I would up to the sky soar,
And sixty deities I would there adore.
Looking down, I am far away from you,
You wave to me, wretched with a mute rue.

* Mingts'o Yin: a friend of Pai Li's, an orthographer and then a granary officer.
* T'iao Hsieh: T'iao Hsieh (A.D. 464 - A.D. 499), an outstanding landscape poet, a highborn aristocrat in Southern and Northern Dynasties period.
* Hsieh the poet: Lingyün Hsieh (A.D. 385 - A.D. 433) in full name, a highborn poet, Buddhist and traveler, famous for landscape poems.
* five colors: referring to five major colors: blue, red, white, black and yellow; a metonymy for various colors, like *The Word and the World* says: "Five colors dazzle the eyes, five sounds deafen the ears, five tastes baffle the palate, galloping to hunt drives one crazy, and rare goods reduce one to misconduct."
* deer: a ruminant (family *Cervidae*), having deciduous antlers, usually in the male only, as the moose, elk, and reindeer. Deer are closely related to Chinese life. Deer hide is a precious gift, especially presented to a female and a deer is usually a symbol of imperial power as it is often a target of pursuit.
* ganoderma: Ganoderma Lucidum Karst in Latin, a grass with an umbrella top, a pore fungus, used as medicine and tonic in China.
* Ssuma: Hsiangju Ssuma (179 B.C.- 118 B.C.) in full name, a representative verse writer in Chinese literary history.
* Kung Wang: Kung Wang (? - A.D. 398), a renowned scholar in the Eastern Chin dynasty. He used to wear a crane cloak in snowy days, which amazed the people with his dignified bearing.
* The Heaven Pool: a fairy pool on Mt. Queen, by which Mother West held banquets.

临 路 歌

大鹏飞兮振八裔,
中天摧兮力不济。
馀风激兮万世,
游扶桑兮挂石袂。
后人得之传此,
仲尼亡兮谁为出涕。

A Roc Song

The roc flies up, o the eight bounds it quakes;
Tired in the air, from wing to wing it shakes.
Its tale inspires o for ten thousand years;
The mulberry tree o its left sleeve tears.
Offspring know this and pass it thereby;
Confucius died, o who on earth will for it cry?

* roc: a legendary enormous powerful bird of prey. In Chinese mythology, it was transformed from a fish in North Sea. *Sir Lush* reads like this: There in North Sea is a fish called Minnow, whose body spans about a thousand miles. When transformed into a bird, it is called Roc, whose back spans about a thousand miles. With a burst of vigor, it flies up, whose wings are like clouds hemming the sky. This bird, skimming tides, flies to South Sea. And this South Sea is called the Pool of Heaven.
* mulberry: the edible, berry-like fruit of a tree (genus *Morus*) whose leaves are valued for silkworm culture, and the tree itself.
* Confucius: Confucius (551 B.C. - 479 B.C.), a renowned thinker, educator and statesman in the Spring and Autumn period, born in the State of Lu, who was the founder of Confucianism and who had exerted profound influence on Chinese culture.

Confucius is one of the few leaders who based their philosophy on the virtues that are required for the day-to-day living. His philosophy centered on personal and governmental morality, correctness of social relationships, justice and sincerity.

古　　意

君为女萝草，
妾作菟丝花。
轻条不自引，
为逐春风斜。
百丈托远松，
缠绵成一家。
谁言会面易，
各在青山崖。
女萝发馨香，
菟丝断人肠。
枝枝相纠结，
叶叶竞飘扬。
生子不知根，
因谁共芬芳。
中巢双翡翠，
上宿紫鸳鸯。
若识二草心，
海潮亦可量。

Feeling the Past

You are golden trailer to flush;
I am yellow dodder to blush.
So supple creepers we are here;
But in a spring wind do we veer.
I wish to creep onto a pine

So that I can there fast entwine.
Who says we can meet so oft,
Divided by the cliff aloft?
You, trailer sweet, happily play;
I, sweet dodder, worriedly pray.
Your twigs do sway from side to side;
My leaves do fly, more pride, less pride.
My seed does not know where am I;
With whom do you share your supply?
Two kingfishers live in their nest;
Mandarin ducks in their pool rest.
If you have heart-to-heart pleasure,
E'en sea water you could measure.

* dodder: a leafless twining herb of the genus *Cuscuta*, parasitic on several other plants to which it adheres by suckers, very harmful to crops like the soya bean.
* trailer: Trailers and creepers are usually used as metaphors for wives, because they crawl on something, like a wife leaning on her husband.
* kingfisher: a beautiful bird looking like a halcyon pileata.
* mandarin ducks: web-footed, short-legged, broad-billed water birds that always appear in loving pairs, a metaphor for couples in Chinese culture.

山鹧鸪词

苦竹岭头秋月辉，
苦竹南枝鹧鸪飞。
嫁得燕山胡雁婿，
欲衔我向雁门归。
山鸡翟雉来相劝，
南禽多被北禽欺。
紫塞严霜如剑戟，
苍梧欲巢难背违。
我今誓死不能去，
哀鸣惊叫泪沾衣。

Hill Partridges

The Bitter Bamboo Range sees the moon bright;
The bitter bamboo branch sees partridges flight.
A young one's wed to one of the wild geese;
The wild goose will take her home with a breeze.
A pheasant comes to stop her with good words;
Southern birds are bullied by northern birds.
Purple Pass is like a sharp sword, so chill;
A Chinese phoenix tree sways 'gainst your will.
"I would not go with him e'en if I die."
So saying, tears on her clothes, she does cry.

* the Bitter Bamboo Range: a range to the south of Autumn Shore in today's Anhui Province, where Pai Li's former reading room was located.

* partridge: a kind of small, plump-bodied gallinaceous game bird, having white spots on the chest, a symbol of lovesickness in Chinese culture, as it utters a cry sounding like: "bro-bro, no-go-go".
* wild goose: an undomesticated goose that is caring and responsible, taken as a symbol of benevolence, righteousness, good manner, wisdom, and faith in Chinese culture.
* pheasant: a long-tailed gallinaceous bird noted for the gorgeous plumage of the male.
* Purple Pass: referring to the northern land where grass is purple.

历阳壮士勤将军名思齐歌

历阳壮士勤将军,神力出于百夫,则天太后召见,奇之,授游击将军,赐锦袍玉带,朝野荣之。后拜横南将军。大臣慕义,结十友,即燕公张说、馆陶公郭元振为首。余壮之,遂作诗。

太古历阳郡,
化为洪川在。
江山犹郁盘,
龙虎秘光彩。
蓄泄数千载,
风云何霮䨴!
特生勤将军,
神力百夫倍。

A Song of General Ch'in, a Gallant from Leeshine

General Ch'in, a gallant from Leeshine, so powerful, can match a hundred strong men combined. The Dowager felt so surprised when summoning him that she granted him the title General Guerrilla besides a brocade gown and a jade belt. He was honored within and without the court and was later given the title General South Sweeping. His colleagues admired him and made friends with him. He had ten best friends including Yüeh Chang, i.e. Lord of Yan, and Chenyüan Kuo, i.e. Lord Kuant'ao. I feel proud of him, hence the poem.

Leeshine does trace back a long time,

When a lake appears in the clime.
Here hills zigzag, and rills flow deep,
Where tigers and dragons can creep.
He's been nurtured for a thousand years;
Now proper chance for him appears.
General Ch'in, you are born this hour;
A hundred men you can o'erpower.

* Leeshine: It is the hub of roads and waterways between the Long River and the Huai River, with a rich historic legacy such as Soul Shrine of Overlord Yü Hsiang, Yün Wu's Lane, Yarn Washer's Shrine and so on, in today's Ho County, Anhui Province.
* Yüeh Chang: Yüeh Chang (A.D. 667 - A.D. 730), a statesman, prime minister and litterateur in the T'ang dynasty, entitled Lord of Yan.
* Chenyüan Kuo: Chenyüan Kuo (A.D. 656 - A.D. 713), a famous commander and prime minister in the T'ang dynasty, entitled Lord Kuant'ao.
* tigers and dragons: a metaphor for talents.

草 书 歌 行

少年上人号怀素，
草书天下称独步。
墨池飞出北溟鱼，
笔锋杀尽中山兔。
八月九月天气凉，
酒徒词客满高堂。
笺麻素绢排数箱，
宣州石砚墨色光。
吾师醉后倚绳床，
须臾扫尽数千张。
飘风骤雨惊飒飒，
落花飞雪何茫茫！
起来向壁不停手，
一行数字大如斗。
怳怳如闻神鬼惊，
时时只见龙蛇走。
左盘右蹙如惊电，
状同楚汉相攻战。
湖南七郡凡几家，
家家屏障书题遍。
王逸少，张伯英，
古来几许浪得名。
张颠老死不足数，
我师此义不师古。
古来万事贵天生，
何必要公孙大娘浑脱舞。

A Song of Cursive Script

A young talented monk, Hold Plain by name,
With his cursive enjoys unique worldwide fame.
Into your ink pool whales from North Sea fly;
Due to your brush all hares in the hills die.
The eighth moon, the ninth moon, the autumn's chill;
Drinkers and poets come and your whole hall fill.
Hemp paper, silk scrolls are stuffed in chests there,
And from Hsuan there arrive the ink slabs rare.
My master, don't on the rope bed lie drunk,
Get up to write a thousand scrolls, great monk!
Like wind, like thunder, like a sweeping sough;
Like snow, like flurry, like a towering brow.
You just write without stop, facing the wall;
A line of characters make bushels small.
They seem to have seen a demon or ghost,
Who can come up with many, more and most.
The stroke does dash here and there, left and right,
Like Ch'u and Han so engaged in their fight.
Seven counties in Hunan your works boast;
Your scrolls and scripts all families love most.
Master Wang and Saint Chang, all in vain;
How many years have they enjoyed their gain?
My friend, now old, you should not have felt shame;
My master, with you none could be the same.
As of yore, all talents are born, not made;
Why do you need Auntie Lordson's naked masquerade?

* Hold Plain: Hold Plain (A.D. 737 - A.D. 799), a renowned calligrapher and monk in the T'ang dynasty, famous for his cursive script.
* cursive: Cursive script originated from clerical script in the Han dynasty, and with the incorporation of regular script by Right General Wang, his son and others in the Way and Chin dynasties and the development of Hold Plain in the T'ang dynasty has evolved to what it is now.
* whale: a giant cetaceous mammal of fish-like form, especially one of the larger pelagic species, as distinguished from dolphins and porpoises. Whales have the fore limbs developed as broad flattened paddles, hind limbs degenerated, and a thick layer of fat or blubber immediately beneath the skin. A whale is a symbol of great ambition, fortitude and uniqueness.
* hare: a rodent (genus *Lepus*) with cleft upper lip, long ears, and long hind legs, characterized by its timidity and swiftness, habitating woodland, farmland or grassland.
* Master Wang: referring to Hsichih Wang (A.D. 303 - A.D. 379), aslo known as Right General Wang, a highborn calligrapher in the Eastern Chin dynasty, regarded as the Sage of Handwriting.
* Saint Chang: referring to Chih Chang (? - A.D. 192), a renowned calligrapher in the Eastern Chin dynasty and the founder of cursive script.
* My friend: referring to Hsu Chang (A.D. 675 - A.D. 750), a renowned calligrapher in the T'ang dynasty, whose cursive script enjoys one of the highest appreciation along with Pai Li's poem and P'ei Min's sword dance.
* Auntie Lordson's Dance of Blade: Auntie Lordson is a top dancer in the T'ang dynasty, famous for her blade dance. According to historical records, Chang Hsu improved his cursive script with the moves of Auntie Lordson's blade dance.

和卢侍御通塘曲

君夸通塘好，
通塘胜耶溪。
通塘在何处，
远在寻阳西。
青萝袅袅挂烟树，
白鹇处处聚沙堤。
石门中断平湖出，
百丈金潭照云日。
何处沧浪垂钓翁，
鼓棹渔歌趣非一。
相逢不相识，
出没绕通塘。
浦边清水明素足，
别有浣沙吴女郎。
行尽绿潭潭转幽，
疑是武陵春碧流。
秦人鸡犬桃花里，
将比通塘渠见羞。
通塘不忍别，
十去九迟回。
偶逢佳境心已醉，
忽有一鸟从天来。
月出青山送行子，
四边苦竹秋声起。
长吟白雪望星河，
双垂两足扬素波。
梁鸿德耀会稽日，

宁知此中乐事多。

A Poem of Tung Pond in Reply to Vice Imperial Inspector

You praise Tung Pond: It's like a dream,
Much better than the Prajna Stream.
Where is Tung Pond, where is it, where?
It's west of Bankshine, over there.
The trailers creep around the misty tree;
The pheasants flock on the sand dike, so free.
The banks rise and a lake appears on high;
The pool shows the sun and clouds in the sky.
A fisherman angles on ripples blue,
Beating his oar, singing, a hermit true.
No travelers he meets he knows;
Turning about, around he goes.
Lo, water gurgles past her tender feet;
Wow, that's the washing girl from Wu, so sweet.
The blue water flows on and turns about;
It might come here from Fairyland, I doubt.
The Ch'in folks, hens and dogs in peach trees loom;
Compared with Tung Pond, they can only gloom.
To go off from Tung Pond we hate;
Nine out of ten times we're back late.
In such a good place, my heart would fly high;
Suddenly, a bird alights from the sky.
For vagrants the moon appears from the hill;
Bitter bamboos there sing an autumn trill.
Crooning *White Snow* towards the Milky Way,

　　　　Dangling our two feet, the blue waves we play.
　　　　When Swan Liang at Mt. Summit did abide,
　　　　Did he know we'd have fun here side by side?

* the Prajna Stream: a stream located in today's Shaohsing, Chechiang Province, which is said to be the place where the belle West Maid did her laundry.
* pheasant: a long-tailed gallinaceous bird noted for the gorgeous plumage of the male.
* the washing girl from Wu: referring to West Maid, one of the Four Belles in ancient China.
* Fairyland: an ideal abode for immortals, sometimes thought of as being in the middle of East Sea, sometimes in the sky.
* The Ch'in folk, hens and dogs in peach trees loom: According to Poolbright T'ao's writing, a group of Ch'in people fled to Peach Blossom Source to keep away from the turbulent days, and the people and their offsprings had lived an idyllic and isolated life for 500 years before a fisherman of Chin strayed into the village.
* peach: any tree of the genus *Prunus Percica*, blooming brilliantly and bearing fruit, a fleshy, juicy, edible drupe.
* *White Snow*: a song representing a highbrow work.
* the Milky Way: a luminous band circling the heavens composed of stars and nebulae; the Galaxy.
* Swan Liang: a hermit and poet in the Eastern Han dynasty.
* Mt. Summit: the K'uaichi Mountains in present-day Chechiang Province, where Worm convened a summit attended by vassal lords, hence the name.

古近体诗四十三首
Old-new Rhythmic Poetry, 43 Poems

赠 孟 浩 然

吾爱孟夫子，
风流天下闻。
红颜弃轩冕，
白首卧松云。
醉月频中圣，
迷花不事君。
高山安可仰，
徒此揖清芬。

To Haojan Meng

Old Meng, your mode I do revere;

Your romance all the world can hear.

In prime, ranks and fame you did spurn;

Gray-haired, to pine woods you'd return.

You drink to inebriate the moon;

Amid blooms, you won't serve the throne.

The peak's too high to look up to;

I can but bow to your pure dew.

* Haojan Meng: Haojan Meng (A.D. 689 – A.D. 740), a renowned pastoral poet, Pai Li's good friend, ranking next to Pai Li and Fu Tu in the entire galaxy of the poets of the glorious T'ang Empire, but unfulfilled officially, he lived in reclusion almost all his life.
* Old Meng: Haojan Meng. Pai Li used a term of endearment or kindly familiarity to show their solidarity.
* the moon: the celestial body that revolves around the earth from west to east as a satellite, which appears at night and gives off shining silvery light, an image of purity and solitude in Chinese culture.

赠从兄襄阳少府皓

结发未识事，
所交尽豪雄。
却秦不受赏，
击晋宁为功。
托身白刃里，
杀人红尘中。
当朝揖高义，
举世称雄风。
小节岂足言，
退耕春陵东。
归来无产业，
生事如转蓬。
一朝乌裘敝，
百镒黄金空。
弹剑徒激昂，
出门悲路穷。
吾兄青云士，
然诺闻诸公。
所以陈片言，
片言贵情通。
棣华倘不接，
甘与秋草同。

To My Cousin, County Inspector of Sowshine

Too naive to know the world then,

I went along with gallant men.
I helped others, not to be praised,
Nor did I fight to be high raised.
With my sharp sword I used to kill;
And I slaughtered rascals at will.
We friends did what was deemed as right,
Praised by all for our heroic might.
These trifles should be laid aside;
East of Poundridge we will abide.
Back home I've nothing to live on,
Blown here and there like thistledown.
The fur I then wore is now rent;
The hundred bars of gold I've spent.
Once I did myself recommend;
I've come all the way to the end.
Now, cousin, you've a good career,
With much gold, having joined the peer.
Now in such a state I have been;
No more words, you know what I mean.
If you could not give me a hand,
I'd be blown like grass o'er the land.

* Poundridge: a vassal state of Han, northwest of present-day Peacefar (Ningyüan), Hunan Province.
* thistledown: the pappus of a thistle, a kind of vigorous prickly plant with cylindrical or globular heads of tubular purple flowers, an important image in Chinese Literature, a symbol of helpless vagrancy or straying.

淮海对雪赠傅霭

朔雪落吴天，
从风渡溟渤。
梅树成阳春，
江沙浩明月。
兴从剡溪起，
思绕梁园发。
寄君郢中歌，
曲罢心断绝。

Singing in Snow to Ai Fu in Huaihai

To Wu Land whirls the northern snow;
To East Sea the wind does it blow.
The plums burst, blooms red, snow white,
River and shoal neath the moon bright.
Hence occurs to me the Shan Stream,
And you in Liang's Park haunt my dream.
Now I sing *Sunlit Snow* to you,
And then I'm choked with a sad rue.

* Wu Land: a vague term for the southern part of China, mainly the area governed by the State of Wu and East Wu founded by Ch'üan Sun.
* East Sea: what is now East China Sea, with an area of 770 thousand square kilometers.
* plum: a kind of plant or the edible purple drupaceous fruit of the plant which is any one of various trees of the genus *Prunus*, cultivated in temperate zones.
* the Shan Stream: a main stream with rich cultural attractions in present-day Shengchow, Chechiang Province.

* Liang's Park: also called Prince Liang's Park, a royal park established by Prince Piety of Liang in the Western Han dynasty, located in the ruins of the State of Sung, that is, today's Shangch'iu, Honan Province, the birthplace of Sir Lush, one of the forerunners of Wordism.
* *Sunlit Snow*: songs including *Sunlit Spring* and *White Snow*, which represent highbrow works.

赠徐安宜

白田见楚老，
歌咏徐安宜。
制锦不择地，
操刀良在兹。
清风动百里，
惠化闻京师。
浮人若云归，
耕种满郊歧。
川光净麦陇，
日色明桑枝。
讼息但长啸，
宾来或解颐。
青橙拂户牖，
白水流园池。
游子滞安邑，
怀恩未忍辞。
翳君树桃李，
岁晚托深期。

To Hsu, the Magistrate of Peace

In White Farm many folks I saw;
They praised you while standing in awe.
Governance you are so good at,
Not fussy but able like that.
Your merit's to the county known,

Spreading even to the throne.
People come on from all around
To till barren fields or bare ground.
The wheat farm is brilliantly shone;
The mulberries bask in the sun.
At disputes you raise your just voice;
With visitors you share your joys.
Oranges by the window well yield,
And you draw water to the field.
I've come to Peace for a short stay;
So helped, I'm shy to go away.
With your grace I don't feel ignored;
Please recommend me to the Lord.

* Peace: a township now belonging to Yangchow, Chiangsu Province, with a total area of 102 square kilometers.
* White Farm: White Farm Ford in today's Yangchow, Chiangsu Province.
* wheat: a grain yielding an edible flour, the annual product of a cereal grass (genus *Triticum*), introduced to China from West Asia more than 4,000 years ago, used as a staple food in China and most of the world. In its importance to consumers, it is second only to rice.
* mulberry: the edible, berry-like fruit of a tree (genus *Morus*) whose leaves are valued for silkworm culture, and the tree itself, first cultivated in the drainage area of the Yellow River in China about five thousand years ago, concurrent with the time when silkworms were raised.
* orange: a reddish, yellow, round, edible citrus fruit, with a sweet, juicy pulp; any of various evergreen trees (genus *Citrus*) of the rue family bearing this fruit.

赠任城卢主簿潜

海鸟知天风，
窜身鲁门东。
临觞不能饮，
矫翼思凌空。
钟鼓不为乐，
烟霜谁与同。
归飞未忍去，
流泪谢鸳鸿。

To Secretary Lu of Jen

The sea bird that feels a wind high
To the east of Lu's gate does fly.
It could not drink wine from the cup
And would flap its wings to fly up.
Lutes and flutes cannot make it cheer;
Who will with it haze and mist share?
It feels it hard to go from here;
To the geese and ducks it sheds tear.

* It could not drink wine from the cup: an allusion to a fable in *Sir Lush*, the beginning of which reads like this: Once, a sea bird took a rest in a suburb of Lu, and the Lord of Lu had it caught and kept in the Royal Shrine. He tried to please it with the royal music of *Fair* and feed it with offerings of Grand Bull. The sea bird felt dizzy and sad, not daring to eat a morsel of meat or drink a cup of wine.
* goose: one of a subfamily (*Anserinae*) of wild or domesticated web-footed birds larger than ducks and smaller than swans, usually a sign of good luck because of its red

protruding head.
* duck: a web-footed, broad-billed water bird of the *Anatinae* family comprising fresh water and wood ducks, the sea and bay ducks, and the mergansers, the quack-crack of which makes it a symbol of success in passing Grand Test, i.e., the imperial civil examination in ancient China.

早秋赠裴十七仲堪

远海动风色,
吹愁落天涯。
南星变大火,
热气馀丹霞。
光景不可回,
六龙转天车。
荆人泣美玉,
鲁叟悲匏瓜。
功业若梦里,
抚琴发长嗟。
裴生信英迈,
屈起多才华。
历抵海岱豪,
结交鲁朱家。
复携两少女,
艳色惊荷葩。
双歌入青云,
但惜白日斜。
穷溟出宝贝,
大泽饶龙蛇。
明主倘见收,
烟霞路非赊。
时命若不会,
归应炼丹砂。

To Chung K'an P'ei Seventeen in Early Autumn

From the sea there blows a wind high,
Blowing my sadness to the sky.
The southern star brings in much heat
That makes clouds with colors replete.
We can't bring time back to the start;
The six dragons turn the Sky Cart.
Over the jade the Chaste man cried;
Over the gourd the Lu folk sighed.
By far for gains I've wished in vain;
Stroking the lute, I sigh with pain.
Sir, what a great hero you are!
You are like a bright rising star.
Now you have travelled the Mid-land
And got along well with peers grand.
With two girls you go on a trip,
Whose colors cause lotus buds to tip.
Their songs rise and with the clouds run;
They hate the setting of the sun.
Bright pearls come from the oceans deep;
In wild swamps snakes and dragons creep.
If favored by the Lord one day,
You will rise and go your broad way.
If you've no chance for grants divine,
Just come, let's cinnabar refine.

* the Sky Cart: referring to the sun, which is driven by a six-dragoned cart in Chinese

myths.
* the Chaste man: referring to Ho Pian who failed twice and lost his legs in an attempt to present crude jade stone he found in Mt. Chaste to monarchs of Ch'u before Lord Civil of Ch'u's enthronement. Ho held the jade stone, crying bitterly for the previous misjudgment. Up to this point, the precious jade was appreciated by the new lord.
* the Lu folk: referring to the poet himself, who now stays in Lu. The poet sees the guard as himself for neither of them has been well-assigned.
* lotus: one of the various plants of the waterlily family, characterized by their large floating round leaves and showy flowers, especially the white or pink Asian lotus, used as a religious symbol in Hinduism and Buddhism. In Chinese culture, it is a symbol of purity and elegance, unsoiled though out of soil, so clean with all leaves green, is a common image in Chinese literature, as two lines of a lyric by Hsiu Ouyang (A.D. 1007-A.D. 1072) read: "A thunder brings rain to the wood and pool, / The rain hushes the lotus, drips cool."
* pearl: a lustrous, calcareous concretion deposited in layers around a central nucleus in the shells of various mollusks, and largely used as a gem, medicine or given as a gift to represent love and friendship.
* snake: an ophidian reptile, having a greatly elongated, scaly body, no limbs, and a specialized swallowing apparatus, a symbol of indifference, malevolence, cattiness, and craftiness in Chinese culture.
* cinnabar: a crystallized red mercuric sulfide, HgS, the chief ore of mercury, the raw mineral material for elixir in Wordist alchemy.

赠范金卿二首

To Fan, the Magistrate, Two Poems

其 一

君子枉清盼，
不知东走迷。
离家来几月，
络纬鸣中闺。
桃李君不言，
攀花愿成蹊。
那能吐芳信，
惠好相招携。
我有结绿珍，
久藏浊水泥。
时人弃此物，
乃与燕珉齐。
摭拭欲赠之，
申眉路无梯。
辽东惭白豕，
楚客羞山鸡。
徒有献芹心，
终流泣玉啼。
祗应自索漠，
留舌示山妻。

No. 1

You are detached in vain, my sir;

You can't tell a hide from a fur.
For months I've been here in the town;
Crickets chirp to my wife's sad frown.
Peaches and plums ne'er e'er speak;
Their blooms or fruit all come to seek.
Your worth you don't have to speak out;
Your good conscience all know about.
An emerald jewel not to spoil,
I'll bury it deep in the soil.
Though everyone does it despise,
I would make it a sacrifice.
I stroke it with care, up and down;
I've no way to give it to Crown.
One in Liao gave Him a pig white,
And one in Ch'u a pheasant bright!
Though I do have a treasure real,
I cry I could not spend the zeal.
So I go back to my hometown,
And show my tongue to my wife's frown.

* cricket: a leaping orthopterous insect, with long antennae and three segments in each tarsus, the male of which makes a chirping sound by friction of forewings, a common image of a quiet night in Chinese literature.
* plums and peaches: a metonymy for plants in general; a metaphor for disciples or students, and sometimes symbolizing a flashy life.
* Ch'u: the State of Ch'u, a large vassal state under Chough, one of the powers in the Warring States period, conquered and annexed by Ch'in in 223 B.C.
* pheasant: a long-tailed gallinaceous bird noted for the gorgeous plumage of the male.

其 二

范宰不买名，
弦歌对前楹。
为邦默自化，
日觉冰壶清。
百里鸡犬静，
千庐机杼鸣。
浮人少荡析，
爱客多逢迎。
游子睹嘉政，
因之听颂声。

No. 2

Magistrate, you buy no vain things;
To the columns, you pluck the strings.
You rule the folks with no ado,
Like a kettle that shines with hue.
Your county, so peaceful, does boom;
Every wife works her busy loom.
No loafers you see in the street;
All give their guest a copious treat.
I, so moved with what you have done,
Sing high praise of you, a good one.

---

* You rule the folks with no ado: an allusion to *The Word and the World*, which reads: Therefore, the sage says: "If I do nothing, the people can raise themselves; if I stay quiet, they can provide for themselves; if I do no fuss, they will become well off; if I have no greed, a simple life they will lead."

赠瑕丘王少府

皎皎鸾凤姿,
飘飘神仙气。
梅生亦何事,
来作南昌尉。
清风佐鸣琴,
寂寞道为贵。
一见过所闻,
操持难与群。
毫挥鲁邑讼,
目送瀛洲云。
我隐屠钓下,
尔当玉石分。
无由接高论,
空此仰清芬。

To Wang, a Sheriff of Spotknoll

Pure, pure like a white crane so fair,
You seem to ride a divine air.
With Plum Blessing you can compare;
Why just be a sheriff down here?
You pluck your lute in the wind clear,
And in calmness hold the Word dear.
You judge well what you see and hear,
Keeping away from a bad peer.
With your brush, all disputes you clear,

Seeing clouds eastward disappear.
I'm with fishers and butchers here;
You should tell jadeite from stone mere.
I can't talk with you over there,
Your grace and fragrance I revere.

* Spotknoll: an ancient fief in today's Yanchow, Shantung Province.
* crane: one of a family of large, long-necked, long-legged, heronlike birds allied to the rails, a symbol of integrity and longevity in Chinese culture, only second to the phoenix in cultural importance.
* Plum Blessing: Mei Fu if transliterated, a magistrate in the Western Han dynasty, who lived in seclusion when in a turbulent age, and he's said to have become an immortal.
* the Word: referring to Tao if transliterated, the most significant and profoundest concept in Chinese philosophy. The Word is identifiable with the Word or Logos in the West, as there is an enormous amount of common ground in the two cosmologies and the doctrines concerning the most fundamental matters such as "the Word is the One" and "God is the One", and the personalization of Being, the progenitor of finite spirits, which are subordinate kinds of Beingor merely appearances of the Divine, the One.

东鲁见狄博通

去年别我向何处，
有人传道游江东。
谓言挂席度沧海，
却来应是无长风。

Seeing Broadcom Ti in East Lu

We parted last year, and where are you gone?
I hear east of the River you stroll on.
And it's said across the ocean you sail,
Sailing before the wind, so calm, o hail.

* Broadcom Ti: Jenchieh Ti's great grandson, a friend of Pai Li's.
* the River: referring to the Yellow River.

见京兆韦参军量移东阳二首

Seeing Staff Wei Moved from Capital to Eastshine, Two Poems

其 一

潮水还归海，
流人却到吴。
相逢问愁苦，
泪尽日南珠。

No. 1

All tides and ebbs for the ocean,
You're in Wu for your demotion.
As we've met, we exchange our woe;
Our tears like pearls endlessly flow.

* Wu: referring to the area south of the Yangtze River, where the State Wu and East Wu had their day.
* Eastshine: established as a county in A. D. 195, in today's Chinhua, Chechiang Province.
* pearl: a smooth, lustrous, usually white and bluish-gray, calcareous concretion deposited in layers around a central nucleus in the shells of various mollusks or oysters, and largely used as a gem, medicine or given as a gift, representing nobility, purity and dignity in Chinese culture.

其 二

闻说金华渡，
东连五百滩。
全胜若耶好，
莫道此行难。
猿啸千溪合，
松风五月寒。
他年一携手，
摇艇入新安。

No. 2

The Golden Flora Ford, I hear,
Links up with Five-hundred Shoal there.
Than Prajna it's a better view;
Don't say it's a hard way to go.
On far-going banks monkeys shrill;
In the fifth moon, pines are still chill.
The next year hand in hand we'll go;
On the New Peace River we'll row.

* the Golden Flora Ford: a ford 2.5 kilometers from Golden Flora (Chinhua), in present-day Chinhua, Chechiang Province.
* Five-hundred Shoal: As said, the shoal is so wide that five hundred people are needed for one batch.
* Prajna: the Joyeh Stream located in Shaohsing, flowing into Lake Mirror, in today's Chechiang Province, which is said to be the place where the belle West Maid did her laundry.
* the New Peace River: located in the upper stretch of the Ch'ient'ang River, deriving from Anhui.

赠丹阳横山周处士惟长

周子横山隐,
开门临城隅。
连峰入户牖,
胜概凌方壶。
时作白纻词,
放歌丹阳湖。
水色傲溟渤,
川光秀菰蒲。
羽化如可作,
相携上清都。
当其得意时,
心与天壤俱。
闲云随舒卷,
安识身有无。
抱石耻献玉,
沉泉笑探珠。

To Staff Chou in the Broadwise Hills in Redshine

Sir, in the Broadwise Hills you hide;
Door opened, you see the town-side.
The ranges stretch on before you;
Eden can't have a better view.
White Ramie verse you often make
And sing aloud to Redshine Lake.

The lake view looms there, coolly nice,
To sway the cattails and wild rice.
When you feel so proud or so high,
Your heart will merge with the blue sky.
When you see free clouds come and go,
You'll forget yourself and your woe.
Your great jadeite you will not show;
You laugh at those who for pearls go.
If one day we could in plumes fly,
We would tour the castles on high.

* the Broadwise Hills: in the northern part of present-day Sha'anhsi Province.
* Redshine: a lake at the lower stretch of the Yangtze River and a county in present-day Chiangsu Province, instituted by Emperor First in 221 B.C., the long history of which has left us a long list of celebrities and rich legacies.
* Eden: the garden that was the first home of Adam and Eve, used as a metaphor for any delightful region or abode, a paradise.
* *White Ramie*: a conservatoire tune, usually played for a Wu dance.
* cattail: a perennial aquatic plant (genus *Typha*), with long leaves, flowers in cylindrical terminal spikes, and downy fruit.
* wild rice: a tall aquatic grass, what is *zizania aquatica* in Latin, the stem of which is used as a vegetable and the grain of which was formerly used as food, now esteemed as a table delicacy.
* pearl: a lustrous, calcareous concretion deposited in layers around a central nucleus in the shells of various mollusks, and largely used as a gem.

玉真公主别馆苦雨赠卫尉张卿二首

Two Poems to Royal Captain Chang at Princess Jade True's Villa in a Rain

其 一

秋坐金张馆,
繁阴昼不开。
空烟迷雨色,
萧飒望中来。
翳翳昏垫苦,
沉沉忧恨催。
清秋何以慰,
白酒盈吾杯。
吟咏思管乐,
此人已成灰。
独酌聊自勉,
谁贵经纶才。
弹剑谢公子,
无鱼良可哀。

No. 1

In the gold house I sit and sigh,
All clouds stagnant over the sky.
The haze spreads to the misty rain;
The sough blows chill air to my pain.
The dark clouds set me in bad mood;
With a heavy heart I do brood.

So chill now, what can cheer me up?
The white spirit filling the cup.
I think of Kuan and Yüeh of yore;
But they are all dust, seen no more.
To comfort myself I drink now;
To the state's talents who will bow?
I draw my sword and sing, alack:
"O sword, no fish to eat, go back."

* Princess Jade True: Princess Jade True (A. D. 692 - A. D. 762), Upmost Truth by Wordist name, a princess and Wordist in the T'ang dynasty, Emperor Sagacious of T'ang's daughter and Emperor Deepsire of T'ang's sister.
* Kuan and Yüeh: referring to Chung Kuan (723 B.C.- 645 B.C.) and Ee Yüeh (? -?). Chung Kuan was a renowned minister of Ch'i in the Spring and Autumn period, and Ee Yüeh a famous commander of Yan in the Warring States period.

其 二

苦雨思白日，
浮云何由卷。
稷契和天人，
阴阳乃骄蹇。
秋霖剧倒井，
昏雾横绝巘。
欲往咫尺途，
遂成山川限。
潨潨奔溜闻，
浩浩惊波转。
泥沙塞中途，
牛马不可辨。
饥从漂母食，
闲缀羽陵简。
园家逢秋蔬，
藜藿不满眼。
螨蛸结思幽，
蟋蟀伤褊浅。
厨灶无青烟，
刀机生绿藓。
投箸解鹡鹉，
换酒醉北堂。
丹徒布衣者，
慷慨未可量。
何时黄金盘，
一斛荐槟榔。
功成拂衣去，
摇曳沧洲傍。

No. 2

O'ercast, I miss a sunny day;
How can I sweep the clouds away?
Corns and Deeds mediate night and day;
But Shade and Shine does not obey.
An autumn rain outflows a flood;
Over the cliffs haze and smoke scud.
To cross the small way it's so hard;
It's by rivers and mountains barred!
The water flows, a rushing sound,
The startled waves turning around.
Silt and sand so heaped by the flood,
One can't tell a cow from a stud.
If hungry, I'll beg for a meal;
To kill time, I read a great deal.
For my life, my vegetable field
Does a bit of lamb's quarters yield.
Cobwebs here and there in the room,
Crickets cheep and chirp to my gloom.
My kitchen stove sends no more smoke;
The kneading board does with moss choke.
I take off my phoenix gown fine
To exchange for some mellow wine.
Tant'u's guy, poverty-stricken,
Had a bright future unshaken.
When I turn out wealthy like him,
Areca nuts filled to the brim?
When I fly with pride, high and higher,
To Blue Shoal there I will retire.

* Corns and Deeds: talents in the age of Hibiscus. Corns taught people on farm work, and Deeds was a minister in charge of civil affairs.
* Shade and Shine: the most important and basic concept of Chinese or Eastern philosophy, characterized by three features: identification, opposition and interconversion.
* cricket: a leaping orthopterous insect, with long antennae and three segments in each tarsus, the male of which makes a chirping sound by friction of forewings, a common image of a quiet night in Chinese literature.
* Tant'u's guy: referring to Muchi Liu (A.D. 360 – A.D. 417), minister from Tant'u in the late Eastern Chin dynasty. Poor in his early age, he used to get mocked by his brother-in-law for asking for areca nuts. When he was promoted, he repaid him with a gold plate of areca nuts.
* Blue Shoal: an ancient town near Rising Bay in today's Hopei Province.

赠韦秘书子春

谷口郑子真，
躬耕在岩石。
高名动京师，
天下皆籍籍。
斯人竟不起，
云卧从所适。
苟无济代心，
独善亦何益。
惟君家世者，
偃息逢休明。
谈天信浩荡，
说剑纷纵横。
谢公不徒然，
起来为苍生。
秘书何寂寂，
无乃羁豪英。
且复归碧山，
安能恋金阙。
旧宅樵渔地，
蓬蒿已应没。
却顾女几峰，
胡颜见云月。
徒为风尘苦，
一官已白须。
气同万里合，
访我来琼都。
披云睹青天，

扪虱话良图。
留侯将绮里,
出处未云殊。
终与安社稷,
功成去五湖。

To Secretary Sirspring Wei

To Dalemouth Sirtruth retires now;
Mid rocks he will start to plough.
All capital men know his name;
All the world sings praise of his fame.
He would not an official be;
Leaning on clouds, he could be free.
If he's no heart for worldly men,
What's the use of loftiness then?
Since you are of the noble line,
You can now serve the lord divine.
Talking of the world you're fluent;
Discussing warfare, you're brilliant.
Lord Hsieh to help the state did rise
And saved all souls under the skies.
A secretary's post is too small;
You can't display your flair at all.
Once to green hills you had resort;
How could you waste your life at court?
Your mansion collapsed to the ground,
Wormwood and grass sprawling around.
You turned around to Girl Seat Peak
That at the clouds and moon did peek.

You have worked so much the hard way;
Now behold, your beard has grown gray.
For us chemistry there must be;
You came to Mt. Lodge to find me.
Donning clouds, we looked at the blue,
And talked of the world, false or true.
Like Chang and Lichi Ch'i combined,
We are the same, of the same mind.
The riotous world once we've settled,
We'll go to Five Lakes, untroubled.

* Sirspring Wei: a counsellor of Prince E'er in the T'ang dynasty.
* Dalemouth: a place 20 kilometers to the west of Cloudshine County in today's Sha'anhsi Province.
* Sirtruth: Sirtruth Cheng, Dalemouth Sirtruth by nick name, a hermit from Dalemouth in the late Western Han dynasty, tilling and reading in the hills, aloof from politics and material pursuits.
* Lord Hsieh: any of the representative figures of the Hsieh's: Hieh An, Lingyün An Hsieh T'iao.
* Girl Seat Peak: 45 kilometers west of Goodshine County in today's Honan Province.
* Mt. Lodge: a famous mountain with many historic, cultural and religious attractions, located in present-day Chianghsi Province.
* Chang: referring to Liang Chang (250 B.C.- 186 B.C.), a prominent statesman and counsellor, and one of the founders of Han. He retired from the center of power as the House of Han was consolidated.
* Lichi Ch'i: one of the Four Old Men, Pang Liu's think tank, a hermit in the early Han dynasty.
* the Five Lakes: referring to Lake T'ai and the other four lakes around. As legend goes, Li Fan (536 B.C.- 448 B.C.), a renowned statesman, strategist, economist and Wordist in the Spring and Autumn period, changed his name to live in seclusion among the Five Lakes after he helped the State of Yüeh wipe out Wu.

赠韦侍御黄裳二首

To Yellowrobe Wei, the Royal Servant, Two Poems

其 一

太华生长松，
亭亭凌霜雪。
天与百尺高，
岂为微飙折？
桃李卖阳艳，
路人行且迷。
春光扫地尽，
碧叶成黄泥。
愿君学长松，
慎勿作桃李。
受屈不改心，
然后知君子。

No. 1

Atop Mt. Flora tall pines grow,
Erect there against frost and snow.
A hundred feet tall, they don't bow;
How can they be felled by a sough?
Different, the peaches and plums smile;
All tourists they try to beguile.
But when spring finishes its stay,
They fall aground and become clay.

May you, like a pine there, stand high,
Not like peaches or plums nearby.
If wronged, stand upright you still can,
You will be known as a real man.

* pine: any of a genus (*Pinus*) of evergreen trees of the pine family, a cone-bearing tree having bundles of two to five needle-shaped leaves growing in clusters, an important image in Chinese literature, a symbol of rectitude, longevity and so on.
* Mt. Flora: one of the Five Sacred Mountains in China, representing the west, regarded as the steepest and saintly mountain in China as it is one of the progenitors of Chinese culture, the shrine of Wordism and the abode of God of Mt. Flora, located in today's Flowershade, Sha'anhsi Province.
* plums and peaches: a metonymy for plants in general; a metaphor for disciples or students, and sometimes symbolizing a flashy life.

其 二

见君乘骢马，
知上太行道。
此地果摧轮，
全身以为宝。
我如丰年玉，
弃置秋田草。
但勖冰壶心，
无为叹衰老。

No. 2

If you're of your piebald astride,
We know to Mt. Great Go you ride.
The bumpy road will harm your wheel;
You should guard yourself a great deal.
I'm like a piece of bumper jade,
In withered autumn grass I'm laid.
Take yourself as an ice pot gold;
Do not sigh because you are old.

* Mt. Great Go: Mt. T'aihang if transliterated, meandering on the border of Shanhsi, Honan and Sha'anhsi.
* ice pot: also referred to as jade pot, a pot crystally bright and clean, usually alluding to the purity of the holder's heart, and sometimes referring to the pure world of immortality, where elixirs are concocted.

赠薛校书

我有吴趋曲，
无人知此音。
姑苏成蔓草，
麋鹿空悲吟。
未夸观涛作，
空郁钓鳌心。
举手谢东海，
虚行归故林。

To Hsüeh, a Book Compiler

I have an air of the Wu State;
But none can it appreciate.
Kusu has fallen into grass;
Elks whine sadly in vain, alas.
I've no chance to offer my *Tide*,
Or catch turtles with a hook plied.
My hand raised, I will leave the sea;
Back to the old woods I will be.

* Kusu: the capital of Wu, what is now Soochow, an important city of today's Chiangsu Province.
* elk: a large deer originally of Asia (genus *Alces*), with palmated antlers and the upper lip forming a proboscis for browsing upon trees.
* *Tide*: a poem intended for the emperor.
* turtle: any of a large and widely distributed order of terrestrial or aquatic reptiles having a toothless beak and a soft body encased in a tough shell into which the head,

tail and four legs may be withdrawn. And it is a tortoise-like beast in Chinese mythology, which is said to be a figure of the sixth son of the dragon, and on whose back tablets of great importance are usually carried.

赠何七判官昌浩

有时忽惆怅，
匡坐至夜分。
平明空啸咤，
思欲解世纷。
心随长风去，
吹散万里云。
羞作济南生，
九十诵古文。
不然拂剑起，
沙漠收奇勋。
老死阡陌间，
何因扬清芬。
夫子今管乐，
英才冠三军。
终与同出处，
岂将沮溺群？

To Boom Ho Seven, a Military Judge

Sometimes I feel disconsolate,
Sitting up at night till so late.
At dawn I howl loud to the sky;
The knots and tangles I'd untie.
With a high wind my heart would go
And disperse the clouds with a blow.

A scribe like Sheng Fu I'd not be;
At ninety there reads books still he.
I would, with my sword, rise to stand
And go kill Hun foes in the sand.
If you stay till old in a lane,
How can you a good name attain?
Now, sir, a real talent you are,
In the army you're a new star.
I'd join you in the battlefield;
How can I to Chang and Ni yield?

* Sheng Fu: Sheng Fu (260 B.C.- 141 B.C.), a former scribe in the Ch'in dynasty who hid some scrolls of *Book of History* lest they be burned.
* Hun: nomadic Asian peoples from north and west, a persistent enemy of China.
* Chang and Ni: referring to Chu Chang and Ni Chieh, hermits in the Spring and Autumn period.

读诸葛武侯传书怀赠长安崔少府叔封昆季

汉道昔云季,
群雄方战争。
霸图各未立,
割据资豪英。
赤伏起颓运,
卧龙得孔明。
当其南阳时,
陇亩躬自耕。
鱼水三顾合,
风云四海生。
武侯立岷蜀,
壮志吞咸京。
何人先见许,
但有崔州平。
余亦草间人,
颇怀拯物情。
晚途值子玉,
华发同衰荣。
托意在经济,
结交为弟兄。
毋令管与鲍,
千载独知名。

To Ts'ui, a Sheriff in the Capital When Reading Bright Chuke's Book

The end of Han saw heroes rise,
Fighting openly or in guise.
Not having taken the whole land,
With separate regimes they'd stand.
Pei Liu would reverse the decline,
And met a mastermind divine.
When in Southshine he did abide,
He farmed, for himself to provide.
Pei Liu went to invite him thrice,
Hence storms and torrents did arise.
Chuke helped Pei Liu in Shu Land
And would the capital command.
Who first recognized Chuke then?
But Chouping Ts'ui, in his ken.
Like him, I am not highly bred,
But I would save the world instead.
Now late I have met you, my friend,
Still young, we'll fight for the same end.
Improve economy we would,
United in our brotherhood.
The friendship between Kuan and Pao
Will last a thousand years and more.

---

* Bright Chuke: Bright Chuke (A.D. 181 – A.D. 234), a statesman and strategist, the prime minister of the Kingdom of Shu in the period of the Three Kingdoms (A.D. 220 – A.D. 265).

* Pei Liu: Pei Liu (A.D. 161 – A.D. 223), a descendant of the royal family of Han, the founding lord of Shu in the Three Kingdoms period.
* a mastermind divine: referring to Bright Chuke. Pei Liu and Chuke had a tight relation as water is to fish.
* Chouping Ts'ui: a friend of Bright Chuke's.
* Kuan and Pao: referring to Chung Kuan (723 B.C.– 645 B.C.) and Shuya Pao (? – 644 B.C.), statesmen and ministers of Ch'i, and true friends to each other.

赠郭将军

将军少年出武威，
入掌银台护紫微。
平明拂剑朝天去，
薄暮垂鞭醉酒归。
爱子临风吹玉笛，
美人向月舞罗衣。
畴昔雄豪如梦里，
相逢且欲醉春晖。

To General Kuo

When young, you were stationed in Martial Might;
Now you guard the palace at Silver Height.
At dawn, with your sword, you worship the throne;
At dusk, on your horse, you're drunk, back alone.
With children you play the lute, by wind blown;
The belles, waving their sleeves, dance to the moon.
Our glory in the past seems like a dream;
Now we have met, let's toast to the spring gleam.

* Martial Might: Wuwei if transliterated, also known as Coolton in history, a prefectural city located in present-day Kansu Province, built by Emperor Martial of Han (156 B.C.-87 B.C.) to garrison the border, so named because Swift Huo defeated Huns and thus showed the martial might of the great Han Empire. It has been prosperous as the hub of the Silk Road and famous for wine brewage, hence styled Grape Wine Town.
* Silver Height: a palace gate.
* the moon: the planet of the earth, which appears at night and gives off shining silvery light, an image of purity and solitude in Chinese culture.

驾去温泉后赠杨山人

少年落魄楚汉间,
风尘萧瑟多苦颜。
自言管葛竟谁许,
长吁莫错还闭关。
一朝君王垂拂拭,
剖心输丹雪胸臆。
忽蒙白日回景光,
直上青云生羽翼。
幸陪鸾辇出鸿都,
身骑飞龙天马驹。
王公大人借颜色,
金璋紫绶来相趋。
当时结交何纷纷,
片言道合惟有君。
待吾尽节报明主,
然后相携卧白云。

To Yang, a Hermit, After Accompanying His Majesty to Flora Pool

When young I was down by the River Han,
Cold shouldered here and there, a wretched man.
My Solomon-like talent who adores?
With long long sighs I waste my time indoors.
Once by His Majesty I were well blessed,
I'd sacrifice my heart, throwing a chest.

Now His grace glows to me like the bright sun;
I spread my wings and fly, a happy one.
Escorting the Lord out of the Swan Gate,
Of a sky horse I sit astride, how great!
All peers and courtiers smile with beams to me;
All gems and ribbons get near in high glee.
How many of them have tried to look kind,
But only you and I share the same mind.
When I've repaid His grace and done my best;
I'd go with you and upon white clouds rest.

* Flora Pool: an imperial hot spring palace on Mt. Black Steed.
* Solomon-like talent: implying Chung Kuan and Bright Chuke. Chung Kuan was a renowned minister of Ch'i in the Spring and Autumn period, and Bright Chuke (A.D. 181 - A.D. 234) a prominent statesman, military strategist, prose writer, and inventor in Chinese history.
* Swan Gate: implying imperial academy.
* sky horse: According to historical records, the sky horse from Kusana is a precious kind. As it sprints, its shoulders swell and it sweats as if bleeding.
* gems and ribbons: implying senior officials.

温泉侍从归逢故人

汉帝长杨苑，
夸胡羽猎归。
子云叨侍从，
献赋有光辉。
激赏摇天笔，
承恩赐御衣。
逢君奏明主，
他日共翻飞。

Meeting My Friend When I Come Back from Royal Hunting

Like Lord Martial in Poplar Park,
Our Lord has a hunting tour gay.
I do follow Him by the pool
And offer a verse with a ray.
He appreciates my work much
And grants me a royal array.
I would recommend you to Him,
So that we could both fly some day.

* Lord Martial: Lord Martial (156 B.C.- 87 B.C.), the seventh emperor of the Han dynasty, a prominent statesman, strategist and poet, who made his empire prosperous in all aspects.
* Poplar Park: Poplar Palace inherited from Ch'in and refurbished in Han, southeast of today's Chouchi County, Sha'anhsi Province.

赠裴十四

朝见裴叔则，
朗如行玉山。
黄河落天走东海，
万里写入胸怀间。
身骑白鼋不敢度，
金高南山买君顾。
徘徊六合无相知，
飘若浮云且西去！

To P'ei Fourteen

I see you, Model P'ei, a glare,
Walking upon Mt. Jade so fair.
You stride from East Sea to the River west,
The ten-thousand-mile landscape in your chest.
The nymph riding White Turtle dare not peer;
Gold like the South Mount cannot make you veer.
Within the six bounds none really knows you;
Drifting like a cloud westward you now go.

* P'ei Fourteen: referring to Cheng P'ei, a friend of Pai Li's and one of the Six Hermits by Bamboo Creek.
* Model P'ei: Model P'ei (A.D. 237 – A.D. 291), a senior official with high reputation in the Three Kingdoms period.
* Mt. Jade: an imaginary mountain, a metaphor used in this poem.
* East Sea: what is East China Sea today, with an area of 770 thousand square kilometers.

* the River: referring to the Yellow River.
* the nymph riding White Turtle: a metaphor used to protrude the charm of the protagonist.
* Gold like the South Mount: a metaphor used to contrast with the value of the the protagonist.

赠崔侍御

黄河三尺鲤，
本在孟津居。
点额不成龙，
归来伴凡鱼。
故人东海客，
一见借吹嘘。
风涛倘相见，
更欲凌昆墟。

To Ts'ui, the Royal Servant

The Yellow River carp feet long,
In the First Ford it used to play.
It failed to be a dragon then,
And came back, with small fish to stay.
My friend, you are here from East Sea
And my bosom friend you have been.
If we do have our chance some day,
We would fly high over Mt. Queen.

* carp: fresh water food fish (*Ciprinus carpiao*), originally of China, now widely distributed in Europe and America, a mascot in Chinese culture, symbolizing great success and harmony. An idiom "a carp jumping over the Dragon Gate" means climbing up the social ladder or succeeding in the imperial civil service examination.
* the First Ford: at the point between the middle and lower reaches of the Yellow River, ten kilometers from Loshine.
* dragon: Though variously understood as a large reptile, a marine monster, a jackal and

so on in Western culture, it has been esteemed as a fabulous serpent-like giant winged animal, a totem of the Chinese nation and a symbol of benevolence and sovereignty in Chinese culture.
* East Sea: today's East China Sea, with an area of 770 thousand square kilometers.
* Mt. Queen: Mt. Kunlun if transliterated, the most sacred mountain in China. It starts from the Eastern Pamir Plateau, stretches across New Land (Hsinchiang) and Tibet, and extends to Chinghai, with an average altitude of 5,500 - 6,000 meters. In Chinese myths, Mt. Queen is where Mother West dwells.

述德兼陈情上哥舒大夫

天为国家孕英才，
森森矛戟拥灵台。
浩荡深谋喷江海，
纵横逸气走风雷。
丈夫立身有如此，
一呼三军皆披靡。
卫青谩作大将军，
白起真成一竖子。

Reporting to Marshal Han Koshu

Heaven made you a pillar of the state,
Your soul like a guarded abyss, profound.
Your plans and schemes spurt out from the blue sea;
Your strides like a thunder shake the great ground.
A man should be like you, established well;
With a shout of yours, all foes flee pell-mell.
Blue Watch, by contrast, was but a small fry;
Rise White, before you, was a common guy.

* Han Koshu: Han Koshu (? - A.D. 757), a senior commander and militarist of the T'ang Empire, descended on his father's side from Turgash chieftains and on his mother's from a well-known Khotanese family.
* abyss: a deep fissure in the earth; bottomless gulf, a metaphor for anything too deep for measurement, especially love or feeling or sadness.
* Blue Watch: Blue Watch (? - 106 B.C.), Ch'ing Wei if transliterated, a renowned

commander in the Western Han dynasty.
* Rise White: Rise White (? - 257 B.C.), Ch'i Pai if transliterated, a representative military strategist in the Warring States Period.

雪谗诗赠友人

嗟予沈迷，
猖獗已久。
五十知非，
古人尝有。
立言补过，
庶存不朽。
包荒匿瑕，
蓄此顽丑。
月出致讥，
贻愧皓首。
感悟遂晚，
事往日迁。
白璧何辜，
青蝇屡前。
群轻折轴，
下沉黄泉。
众毛飞骨，
上凌青天。
萋斐暗成，
贝锦粲然。
泥沙聚埃，
珠玉不鲜。
洪焰烁山，
发自纤烟。
苍波荡日，
起于微涓。
交乱四国，

播于八埏。
拾尘掇蜂,
疑圣猜贤。
哀哉悲夫,
谁察予之贞坚?
彼妇人之猖狂,
不如鹊之强强。
彼妇人之淫昏,
不如鹑之奔奔。
坦荡君子,
无悦簧言。
擢发赎罪,
罪乃孔多。
倾海流恶,
恶无以过。
人生实难,
逢此织罗。
积毁销金,
沈忧作歌。
天未丧文,
其如余何。
妲己灭纣,
褒女惑周。
天维荡覆,
职此之由。
汉祖吕氏,
食其在傍。
秦皇太后,
毒亦淫荒。
蟏蛸作昏,
遂掩太阳。

万乘尚尔，
匹夫何伤。
辞殚意穷，
心切理直。
如或妄谈，
昊天是殛。
子野善听，
离娄至明。
神靡遁响，
鬼无逃形。
不我遐弃，
庶昭忠诚。

Beware of Slander, to My Friend

In wine I madly drown,
Unbridled, up and down.
Fifty now, I repent,
As they used to lament.
It's ne'er too late to mend;
My tale goes without end.
Someone his faults does hide
And with flaws does abide.
With the satire *Moon Rise*,
He to his gray hair sighs.
Everything collapses
As old time elapses.
The jade no flaw contains,
Which a greenbottle stains.
A heap may crash a shell

And sink it to the hell.
All feathers make birds fly,
High and higher to the sky.
Slanders spread here and there
May like a brocade glare.
Pearls buried deep below
Cannot brilliantly glow.
On the mountain flames higher
Start from a speck of fire.
The tides that the sea rip
Start from a trivial drip.
A rumor far and nigh
Will to eight counties fly.
Yan and Yin who were kind
Met a suspicious mind.
How sadly my tear flows;
My faithfulness who sees and who knows?
Those women who curse and lie
Are worse than magpies that loudly cry.
Those women who fuss and kill
Are worse than quails that noisily trill.
Oh, my friend, a good one,
Don't be fooled by the tongue.
Their sins we count as such
Can't be foreseen as much.
Their sins if we will pour,
We couldn't have thought more.
O life, such a mishap,
I've fallen to the trap.
Slander can corrode gold;
My sadness I cannot hold.

Heaven above preside;

Who can spurn me aside?

Tachi destroyed King Chow

Pao Ssu bewitched King Chough.

Their states fell with a din,

All because of their sin.

Empress Lü swayed so wide,

Eechi Li by her side.

Empress T'ien had much lust

With Lao Ai who was unjust.

A rainbow, with dim light,

May eclipse the sun bright.

Lords and peers can't this shun,

Let alone a low one.

Though my words have run out;

My heart's still keen and stout.

If what's said is untrue,

I'll be cursed by the blue.

Master K'uang would listen;

Best Sight's eyes would glisten.

God does have a firm hand;

No ghost can flee His land.

If I were not ignored,

You'd see me faithful, Lord.

* Fifty now, I repent: an allusion to Chü Yüan (585 B.C.- 484 B.C.), a renowned Wordist and senior official of Watch. He recalled his faults in the past 49 years at fifty.
* *Moon Rise*: a satire poem in *The Book of Songs*.
* pearl: a lustrous, calcareous concretion deposited in layers around a central nucleus in the shells of various mollusks, and largely used as a gem.
* eight counties: implying all directions.
* Yan and Yin: referring to Hui Yan (521 B.C.- 481 B.C.), Confucius's most admirable

student, and Boch'i Yin. A student of Confucius's saw Hui Yan eating cooked rice and told Confucius. However Confucius found the truth was that the rice was stained by fallen dust, and Yan did not have the heart to waste it. Boch'i Yin, the eldest son of Chifu Yin, was a significant minister of the Chough House. Boch'i Yin was framed by his stepmother and was driven away by his father. At last, his father found out the truth and invited him back.

* magpie: a corvine bird, having a long and graduated tail, which often makes loud chirps.
* Tachi destroyed King Chow: Tachi, an imperial concubine of King Chow (1075 B.C.-1046 B.C.), the last emperor of Shang. It is said that King Chow spent too much time with Tachi and neglected government affairs, therefore, Shang was overthrown by Chough.
* Pao Ssu bewitched King Chough: Pao Ssu, an imperial concubine of King Dark of Chough (795 B.C.? - 771 B.C.). In order to please Pao Ssu, King Dark ignited the beacons, which were used as an alarm to apprise of enemies' coming, to fool the vassal lords. Once the enemies really attacked, King Dark ignited the beacons again, but nobody believed him as he had fooled them too many times before. So Chough collapsed and King Dark was killed.
* Empress Lü: the first empress of Han, i.e. Pang Liu's wife. It is said that Empress Lü had affairs with Eechi Li.
* Eechi Li: a famous lobbyist, who helped Pang Liu win the world. As is said, he had affairs with Empress Lü.
* Lao Ai: the secret lover of Empress T'ien (mother of the first emperor of Ch'in), pretending to be an eunuch so as to be with her.
* Master K'uang: A famous musician from the State of Chin in the Spring and Autumn period.
* Best Sight: the one who could see tiny things from hundred miles away.

赠参寥子

白鹤飞天书，
南荆访高士。
五云在岘山，
果得参寥子。
肮脏辞故园，
昂藏入君门。
天子分玉帛，
百官接话言。
毫墨时洒落，
探玄有奇作。
著论穷天人，
千春秘麟阁。
长揖不受官，
拂衣归林峦。
余亦去金马，
藤萝同所欢。
相思在何处，
桂树青云端。

To Sir Silence

The white crane sent me news divine；
In South Chaste lives a man so fine.
Atop Mt. Steep five clouds appear；
Sir Silence really abides here.
I start from my land, feeling great,

And smiling, enter your front gate.
From our Lord you have gifts diverse;
All grandees would with you converse.
You wave your brush to write good worth,
Hence a work from Heaven and earth.
Heaven, earth and man you explore,
Hence a good book for all in store.
The post declined, swaying your sleeve,
For mountains and rivers you leave.
And I will take leave of Gold Horse;
Vines and grass will be our resource.
Where on earth can we rest or lie?
The laurel tree looms in the sky.

* Sir Silence: a hermit in the T'ang dynasty.
* crane: one of a family of large, long-necked, long-legged, heronlike birds allied to the rails, a symbol of integrity and longevity in Chinese culture, only second to the phoenix in cultural importance.
* South Chaste: referring to the area covering present-day Hupei and Hunan.
* Mt. Steep: an important fort in history, located in the southwest of Sowshine (Hsiangyang), the River Han to its east.
* Gold Horse: name of a gate of a Han palace, where scholar-officials waited to be summoned.
* laurel: laurus nobilis, an evergreen shrub with aromatic, lance-shaped leaves, yellowish flowers, and succulent, cherry-like fruit, a symbol of glory usually in the form of a crown or wreath of laurel to indicate honor or high merit, especially when one had passed Grand Test in ancient China. In Chinese mythology, there is a laurel tree on the moon, and it would never fall even though Kang Wu has kept cutting it.

赠饶阳张司户燧

朝饮苍梧泉，
夕栖碧海烟。
宁知鸾凤意，
远托椅桐前？
慕蔺岂曩古？
攀嵇是当年。
愧非黄石老，
安识子房贤？
功业嗟落日，
容华弃徂川。
一语已道意，
三山期著鞭。
蹉跎人间世，
寥落壶中天。
独见游物祖，
探元穷化先。
何当共携手，
相与排冥筌。

To Sui Chang, a Household Registrar in Richshine

At dawn I drink at Mt. Green Tree;
At dusk I sleep on the blue sea.
Who knows where a phoenix will be?
On a Chinese parasol tree!

Hsiangju Lin of yore I admire;
For K'ang Chi before I aspire.
I'm not Yellow Stone I feel shame;
How could I know your will and aim?
My career's like the setting sun;
My prime like the flow will be gone.
No more words, we know what we mean;
Let's practice in the mountains green.
I'm lost on earth many a day;
The fairyland's still far away.
Let's explore how things are begun,
Hence we will get close to the One.
Now let's move forward hand in hand,
Freed of all barriers in this land.

* Mt. Green Tree: referring to Mt. Nine Doubts. Mt. Nine Doubts, where Hibiscus was buried, so named because it confuses people with its similar peaks and sights.
* phoenix: In Chinese myths, phoenixes, auspicious birds, unlike ordinary ones, only perch on parasol trees, and only eat bamboo shoots and pearly stone.
* Chinese parasol tree: a tree, *Firmiana simplex* in Latin, of the hibiscus family, native to Asia, growing as tall as 12 metres, having deciduous leaves and small greenish white flowers that are borne in clusters.
* Hsiangju Lin: a renowned statesman and diplomat of the State of Chao.
* K'ang Chi: a thinker, musician and litterateur in the Three Kingdoms period.
* Yellow Stone: a legendary Wordist and a military strategist, who gave Liang Chang *The Art of War*.
* Fairyland: an ideal abode for immortals, thought of as being in the middle of East Sea, sometimes high in the sky.
* the One: a philosophical concept of Wordism, the beginning of all things, as is defined in *Sir Lush*, "In the beginning was the None, having nothing, having no name. Then there arose the One, and nothing was formed yet." And in Laocius's *The Word and the World*: "The sky has gotten the One, hence blue and clear; the earth has gotten the One, hence staid and still." Similarly, in the West, God is the One, Self-subsisting Reality. The One in the West and the One in the East are actually one, identifiable though in different languages.

赠清漳明府侄聿

我李百万叶,
柯条布中州。
天开青云器,
日为苍生忧。
小邑且割鸡,
大刀佇烹牛。
雷声动四境,
惠与清漳流。
弦歌咏唐尧,
脱落隐簪组。
心和得天真,
风俗由太古。
牛羊散阡陌,
夜寝不扃户。
问此何以然,
贤人宰吾土。
举邑树桃李,
垂阴亦流芬。
河堤绕绿水,
桑柘连青云。
赵女不冶容,
提笼昼成群。
缲丝鸣机杼,
百里声相闻。
讼息鸟下阶,
高卧披道帙。
蒲鞭挂檐枝,

示耻无扑挟。
琴清月当户，
人寂风入室。
长啸一无言，
陶然上皇逸。
白玉壶冰水，
壶中见底清。
清光洞毫发，
皎洁照群情。
赵北美佳政，
燕南播高名。
过客览行谣，
因之颂德声。

To Yü, My Nephew, Magistrate of Clearflow

A million leaves of the Li's tree
Dispersed in Midland, all named Li.
My nephew, like a blue-cloud ware,
For the masses' life you do care.
Such a small place is just your try;
Into the broad space you will fly.
Like thunder you've shaken the ground;
Your grace, stream-like, will flow around.
Of Mound's heyday you sing praise now;
Like a hermit the farm you plough.
The folks' hearts have a simple cast,
Like those of the saints in the past.
Cattle and sheep roam on the farm;

No doors are closed at night, no harm.
Why like this, why things like this stand?
Because a saint does rule this land.
The fief teems with peaches and plums;
Their shades go away while balm comes.
The water so green flows around;
The mulberries reach high, sky-bound.
Chao girls about their looks don't care;
With lanterns, they crowd here and there.
They fix silk and they work the loom;
The sound travels far from their room.
No disputes, on doorsteps birds play;
You read a book to pass the day.
A cattail whip's hung on the eaves;
In punishment no one believes.
The bright moon o'er the door one sees;
So quiet, to the room blows a breeze.
You never speak aloud or shout,
Like a kind sage walking about.
You're like a kettle of pure ice;
One can see its bottom, so nice.
So clear, it reveals e'en a hair,
And sheds light on any affair.
Northern folks sing praise of your name;
Southern men broadcast your good fame.
A ballad I happen to hear,
Hence the verse I have composed here.

* Midland: usually referring to today's Honan. It should be China in this poem.
* Mound: Mound (2377 B.C.- 2259 B.C.), Yao if transliterated. Divine and noble, Mound has been regarded as one of Five Lords in ancient China.

* plums and peaches: a metonymy for plants in general; a metaphor for disciples or students, and sometimes symbolizing a flashy life.
* Chao girls: girls from the place that was the State of Chao, generally referring to northern girls.
* silk: the fine, soft, shiny fiber produced by silk worms to form their cocoons, and the thread or fabric made from this fibre is used as material for clothing. And it can be any clothing made of silk.
* cattail: a perennial aquatic plant (genus *Typha*), with long leaves, flowers in cylindrical terminal spikes, and downy fruit.

赠临洺县令皓弟

陶令去彭泽，
茫然太古心。
大音自成曲，
但奏无弦琴。
钓水路非远，
连鳌意何深。
终期龙伯国，
与尔相招寻。

To Brother Hao, Magistrate of Linming

Just like Poolbright T'ao you've resigned;
Peacefulness you're going to find.
A great tune's by nature composed;
The stringless strings you can touch, reposed;
You fish for a giant riverside,
Like Six Turtles caught from the tide.
Brobdingnag looms yonder o'er there;
Yonder o'er there, best you will fare.

* Poolbright T'ao: Yüanming T'ao (A.D. 352 – A.D. 427) if transliterated, a complex figure and a poet of complex poems—a verse writer, poet, and litterateur in the Chin dynasty, and the founder of Chinese idyllism, who was once the magistrate of P'engtse.
* Six Turtles: referring to the turtles carrying Mt. Fairy. In Chinese mythology, there were fifteen giant turtles carrying five fairy mountains in turns in East Sea. But a giant man from the State of Giants on the sea caught six turtles and burnt them for divination. As a result, two mountains drifted to the extreme north and sank into the water, with only three fairy mountains left.

赠郭季鹰

河东郭有道，
于世若浮云。
盛德无我位，
清光独映君。
耻将鸡并食，
长与凤为群。
一击九千仞，
相期凌紫氛。

To Eagle Kuo

Lo, Inword Kuo east of the stream!
Like a free floating cloud you seem.
With your great worth I can't compare;
Only to you pureness does glare.
To vie with chickens, what a shame!
To join phoenixes is your aim.
You would fly nine thousand feet high
To soar across the vast blue sky.

* Eagle Kuo: a friend of Pai Li's. He was named Eagle because an eagle is notable for keen sight and strong flight, usually praised as a hero in Chinese culture.
* Inword Kuo: Inword Kuo (A.D. 128 – A.D. 169), Kuo Yutao if transliterated, a renowned scholar and hermit in the Eastern Han dynasty, who refused to serve the corrupted government and was dedicated to schooling in his hometown.
* phoenix: In Chinese myths, phoenixes, auspicious birds, unlike ordinary ones, only perch on parasol trees, and only eat bamboo shoots and pearly stone.

邺中赠王大，劝入高凤石门山幽居

一身竟无托，
远与孤蓬征。
千里失所依，
复将落叶并。
中途偶良朋，
问我将何行。
欲献济时策，
此心谁见明？
君王制六合，
海塞无交兵。
壮士伏草间，
沉忧乱纵横。
飘飘不得意，
昨发南都城。
紫燕枥下嘶，
青萍匣中鸣。
投躯寄天下，
长啸寻豪英。
耻学琅琊人，
龙蟠事躬耕。
富贵吾自取，
建功及春荣。
我愿执尔手，
尔方达我情。
相知同一己，
岂惟弟与兄。
抱子弄白云，

琴歌发清声。
临别意难尽,
各希存令名。

To Firstborn Wang from Mid-Yeh, Whom I Advise to Retire to Hiphoenix's Mt. Stone Gate

Phew, nothing I can rely on,
Drifting, drifting like thistledown.
The long long drifting to me grieves;
There whirl to me the fallen leaves.
Midway I come 'cross a friend true,
Who asks me what I will next do.
I will spread my idea well planned,
But who can my heart understand?
Now our country seems united,
Not by fierce warfare divided.
All heroes lurk in rambling grass;
Their deep worries would them surpass.
Lonely, lonely, I did feel down,
Yesterday, I left the south town.
Purple Swallow at manger neighs;
Olive Duckweed in the sheath brays.
Under the blue sky I'll abide,
And look for heroes carved with pride.
To learn from Tiller I feel shame,
Although farming was not his aim.
To win, you on yourself depend;
A good means leads to a good end.

I would reach out to take your hand,
As you can my heart understand.
I know you just as you know me;
Dearer than brothers we shall be.
For the white clouds the lute we pluck:
The strings give a clear sound: Luck, luck.
While we are ready to depart,
To strive for pride we can now start.

* Hiphoenix: name of an immortal from Southshine, who once taught in the hills in West T'ang.
* Mt. Stone Gate: a mountain unidentified, probably the Buddhist attraction in today's Huaiju, Peking.
* Tiller: Bright Chuke, the premier of Shu in the Three Kingdoms period, a famous strategist and politician.
* Purple Swallow: a poetic name for fine horses.
* Olive Duckweed: a sword of Emperor Lightmight of Han, implying military forces.

赠华州王司士

淮水不绝涛澜高，
盛德未泯生英髦。
知君先负庙堂器，
今日还须赠宝刀。

To Wang, an Organization Official from Flora

The Huai River surges on from tide to tide;
The great virtues nurture heroes with pride.
I know you'll be a vessel for the shrine;
So I present this sword for you to shine.

* Flora: Flowershade Prefecture in T'ang, in today's Flowershade (Huayin), Sha'anhsi Province, 120 kilometers from Long Peace, with a history of more than 2,300 years and having an important strategic position in history, known as the Passway of Ch'in and Thoroughfare of Eight Provinces.
* the Huai River: one of the seven largest rivers in China, between the Long River and the Yellow River, 1,000 kilometers long.

赠卢征君昆弟

明主访贤逸,
云泉今已空。
二卢竟不起,
万乘高其风。
河上喜相得,
壶中趣每同。
沧洲即此地,
观化游无穷。
水落海上清,
鳌背睹方蓬。
与君弄倒景,
携手凌星虹。

To Lu Brothers, Recruits

The good Lord will have saints employed;
But today the Cloud Fountain remains void.
You two brothers don't get up to fly higher;
His Majesty does your virtues admire.
By the Yellow River we meet with glee;
With the same aim, in Fairyland we'll be.
We don't need to go anywhere at all;
In here we can watch how things rise and fall.
Tides all gone, the sea has become so clear;
Riding whales, to Fairyland we can peer.
Our shadows upside down we can play now;

Let's go to the space and the blue sky plough.

* the Cloud Fountain: the name of a fountain or of a cataract, its location unidentified.
* the Yellow River: the second longest river in China, regarded as the cradle of Chinese civilization. It is 5,464 kilometers long, with a drainage area of 752,443 square kilometers. As legend goes, the river derived from a yellow dragon that, couchant on Midland Plain, ate yellow soil, flooded crops, devoured people and stock, and was finally tamed by Great Worm, the First King of Hsia (cir. 21 B.C.- 16 B.C.).
* pine: any of a genus (*Pinus*) of evergreen trees of the pine family, a cone-bearing tree having bundles of two to five needle-shaped leaves growing in clusters, an important image in Chinese literature, a symbol of rectitude, longevity and so on.
* whale: a cetaceous mammal of fish-like form, especially one of the larger pelagic species, as distinguished from dolphins and porpoises. Whales have the fore limbs developed as broad flattened paddles, hind limbs absent, and a thick layer of fat or blubber immediately beneath the skin. A whale is a symbol of great ambition, fortitude and uniqueness.
* Fairyland: an imaginary ideal abode for immortals, sometimes thought of as being in the middle of East Sea, sometimes high above in the sky.

赠新平少年

韩信在淮阴，
少年相欺凌。
屈体若无骨，
壮心有所凭。
一遭龙颜君，
啸咤从此兴。
千金答漂母，
万古共嗟称。
而我竟何为？
寒苦坐相仍。
长风入短袂，
内手如怀冰。
故友不相恤，
新交宁见矜？
摧残槛中虎，
羁绁鞲上鹰。
何时腾风云，
搏击申所能？

To the Young Man in New Peace

When Hsin Han was then in Huaishade,
He was bullied by a bad fop.
Although he did not have hard bones,
He had a will no one could top.
Once he came across the real Lord,

With a great hail, he jumped to rise.
He repaid Washing Mother kind
And had since enjoyed cheers and whys.
What have I done? What can I be?
The pains and rues I can hardly hold.
The wind blows hard into my sleeves;
Like hard ice, my hands feel so cold.
No old friends of mine would help me,
Nor did new ones lend me a hand.
I'm like a tiger in a cage
Or an eagle tied to a stand.
When can I to the white clouds fly
So what has been planned I can try?

* Hsin Han: a founding commander of the Han regime. He had been poor and shown a good endurance of humiliation. Once a young man made fun of him and forced him to crawl through his legs, and Han did so without changing his expression. When he was not appreciated in pursuit of an official career or good at doing business, Han depended on an elder laundry woman who pitied him and gave him food without expectation of a return.
* Huaishade: the birthplace of Hsin Han, a founding commander of Han, in the hinterland of the northern plain of today's Chiangsu, on the southern bank of the Huai River, hence the name.
* Washing Mother: the elder laundry woman who pitied Hsin Han and gave him food when was downtrodden.
* eagle: a diurnal bird of prey of the family Accipitridae of worldwide distribution, notable for keen sight and strong flight, usually praised as a hero in Chinese culture.

赠崔侍御

长剑一杯酒，
男儿方寸心。
洛阳因剧孟，
访宿话胸襟。
但仰山岳秀，
不知江海深。
长安复携手，
再顾重千金。
君乃輶轩佐，
予叨翰墨林。
高风摧秀木，
虚弹落惊禽。
不取回舟兴，
而来命驾寻。
扶摇应借便，
桃李愿成阴。
笑吐张仪舌，
愁为庄舄吟。
谁怜明月夜，
肠断听秋砧！

To Ts'ui, the Royal Servant

A long sword, and a cup of wine!
We toast to ourselves, your heart and mine.
Like Chümeng from Loshine, the best,

You talk with me, fully expressed.
I but admired your grand mount steep
Now I know your mind is as deep.
In Long Peace I've met my friend old;
Our night talk is precious like gold.
You're a deputy envoy great;
As a royal scribe I now wait.
A tall tree's destroyed by a sough;
By shots a bird's frightened enow.
Now you come while your spirits soar,
As if snow whirling to my door.
When you rise high with a brisk breeze,
Peach and plum will dance with the trees.
We laugh, jeering at Ee Chang's tongue;
We frown, so sad with Hsi Chuang's song.
Who's feeling sad with this chill moon?
The pestling block sings a sad tune.

* Chümeng: a gallant in the Fore-Ch'in period, who often saved people from danger.
* Loshine: Loyang if transliterated, the eastern of the two great cities that served as capitals in the early Chinese dynasties, and second city of the Empire in T'ang times, when it had about 800,000 inhabitants.
* Long Peace: the capital of China in the T'ang dynasty, the metropolis of gold, with 1,000,000 inhabitants, the largest walled city ever built by man, and the capital of today's Sha'anhsi Province. It was the most cultivated and cosmopolitan for sure at that time, and T'ang civilization was at its peak.
* Ee Chang: Ee Chang (? -309 B.C.), a political strategist and diplomat in the Warring States period, who gained his fame by outstanding eloquence.
* Hsi Chuang: a minister of Ch'u in the Warring States period. Though he earned a high position in Ch'u, he never forgot his homeland and groaned in his mother tongue when he was ill.
* the moon: the celestial body that revolves around the earth from west to east as a satellite, which appears at night and gives off shining silvery light, an image of purity and solitude in Chinese culture.

走笔赠独孤驸马

都尉朝天跃马归,
香风吹人花乱飞。
银鞍紫鞚照云日,
左顾右盼生光辉。
是时仆在金门里,
待诏公车谒天子。
长揖蒙垂国士恩,
壮心剖出酬知己。
一别蹉跎朝市间,
青云之交不可攀。
倘其公子重回顾,
何必侯嬴长抱关。

To Adjunct Groom Loncliness

The officer oft gallops home from the court;
A balmy wind blows the blossoms to sway.
The silver saddle and bridle do shine,
A beam to the left, to the right a ray.
I was a royal scribe in Golden Gate,
Waiting for the Lord's summon to the court.
I bowed to the crown for His grace for me;
I would give all I have: means and resort.
Now I waste my time in the streets and lanes,
No access to making friends high and great.
If you, officer, would take care of me,

Why should I, like old Ying Hou, keep the gate?

* Adjunct Groom: an emperor's son-in-law, usually holding the position of guarding the horses of the adjunct carts, hence the name.
* Golden Gate: a palace gate near the national academy in the T'ang dynasty.
* Ying Hou: Ying Hou (? -257 B.C.), a hermit living as a porter of Smooth Gate of the State of Way and became Prince Faithridge's hanger-on, through whom the prince obtained the service of Hai Chu.

赠嵩山焦炼师

嵩丘有神人焦炼师者,不知何许妇人也。又云生于齐梁时,其年貌可称五六十。常胎息绝谷,居少室庐,游行若飞,倏忽万里。世或传其入东海,登蓬莱,竟莫能测其往也。余访道少室,尽登三十六峰,闻风有寄,洒翰遥赠。

二室凌青天,
三花含紫烟。
中有蓬海客,
宛疑麻姑仙。
道在喧莫染,
迹高想已绵。
时餐金鹅蕊,
屡读青苔篇。
八极恣游憩,
九垓长周旋。
卜瓢酌颍水,
舞鹤来伊川。
还归空山上,
独拂秋霞眠。
萝月挂朝镜,
松风鸣夜弦。
潜光隐嵩岳,
炼魄栖云幄。
霓裳何飘飖,
凤吹转绵邈。
愿同西王母,
下顾东方朔。
紫书傥可传,

铭骨誓相学。

To the Woman Alchemist on Mt. Tower

On Mt. Tower there is a woman alchemist, and who she is I don't know. As said, she was born about the time of Ch'i and Liang. She looks like in her fifties or sixties. She often fasts, inhaling through her navel or skin. She abides on Mt. Smallroom Lodge and she walks as if flying, three thousand miles in a flash. As is rumored, she has gone to East Sea and climbed up Mt. Fairyland. But where she is gone nobody knows. I have visited Mt. Smallroom and climbed up Thirty-six Peaks in vain. I hear a wind can send a letter to her, hence this poem.

  The two Rooms tower up to the sky;
  The Bedouin tree blooms thrice on high.
  A Fairyland fairy looms there,
  Looking like Hemp Maid brightly fair.
  Her Word is high, of all dust free;
  Her thought is raised, divine to be.
  On laurel pistils she oft dines;
  Made of green moss, her book shines.
  The eight poles she travels so much;
  The nine bounds she rambles as such.
  With a scoop, from the Ying she drinks;
  On a crane, at the Ee she winks.
  At night she goes back to the hills,
  And alone sleeps on cloudy frills.
  The moon to the wisteria glows;
  The wind to the night zither blows.
  Her glamour is spread on Mt. Tower;

Her spirits stroll in the cloud bower.
Her plumage robe flows up and down;
The wind blows and is thereby blown.
I would come down with Mother West
To see Newmoon East there suppressed.
If you could receive this from me,
I would study the Word with thee.

* Mt. Tower: located in the west of present-day Honan Province, one of the Five Mountains esteemed highly in Chinese culture. It is one of the five sanctuaries of Wordism, and the abode of God of Mt. Tower worshipped by Han Chinese, with an area of 450 square kilometers, consisting of Mt. Greatroom and Mt. Smallroom, having 72 peaks, 350 meters above sea level at the lowest and 1,512 meters at the highest.
* Mt. Smallroom Lodge: a lodge on Mt. Smallroom, one of the mountains that make Mt. Tower, located in present-day Honan Province.
* Mt. Fairyland: a mountain on Fairy Isles at East Sea.
* Thirty-six Peaks: There are thirty-six peaks on one of the mountains of Mt. Tower, i.e., Mt. Smallroom.
* the two Rooms: referring to Mt. Smallroom and Mt. Greatroom, two main mountains that make Mt. Tower.
* Hemp Maid: an alternative name of Maid Flax, a mythical figure, who looks eighteen years old but has claimed to witness three times' drying-outs of East Sea.
* laurel pistil: the seed-bearing organ, the best juicy part of a flowering plant called laurel, which is laurus nobilis in Latin nomination, an evergreen shrub with aromatic, lance-shaped leaves, yellowish flowers, and succulent, cherry-like fruit.
* the Ying: a river derived from Mt. Tower. The River Ying has been regarded as one of the origins of Chinese culture.
* the Ee: a river near Loshine, with many historic attractions alongside.
* wisteria: any of a genus *Wisteria* of woody twining shrubs of the bean family, with pinnate leaves, elongated pods, and handsome clusters of blue, purple, or white flowers.
* Mother West: a sovereign goddess living on Mt. Queen in Chinese myths. She was originally described as human-bodied, tiger-toothed, leopard-tailed and hoopoe-haired, regarded as a goddess in charge of women protection, marriage and procreation, and

longevity.
* Newmoon East: a jocular and witted official serving Lord Martial of Han.
* the Word: referring to Tao if transliterated, the most significant and profoundest concept in Chinese philosophy. According to Laocius's *The Word and the World*: "The Word is void, but its use is infinite. O deep! It seems to be the root of all things."

口号赠杨征君

陶令辞彭泽，
梁鸿入会稽。
我寻高士传，
君与古人齐。
云卧留丹壑，
天书降紫泥。
不知杨伯起，
早晚向关西。

An Oral Impromptu to Yang, a Recruit

Poolbright T'ao from P'engtse resigned;
Swan Liang on Summit lived behind.
Saintly People I have all read;
With the past saints you go ahead.
You rest with white clouds in Red Dale,
When you receive a royal mail.
When will you, a sage, I don't know,
Go through the West Pass and west go?

* Poolbright T'ao: Yüanming Tao (A.D. 352 – A.D. 427) if transliterated, a verse writer, poet, and litterateur in the Chin dynasty, and the founder of Chinese idyllism, who was once the magistrate of P'engtse.
* Swan Liang: Hung Liang if transliterated, a hermit in the Eastern Han dynasty who lived in seclusion on Mt. Summit.
* *Saintly People*: a biographical book on 91 saintly people from the Mound's age to the dynasty of Way.
* Red Dale: a term borrowed from Chao Pao's line: The clouds chase in Red Dale.

上 李 邕

大鹏一日同风起，
扶摇直上九万里。
假令风歇时下来，
犹能簸却沧溟水。
世人见我恒殊调，
闻余大言皆冷笑。
宣父犹能畏后生，
丈夫未可轻年少。

To Yung Li

One day the roc with the wind does arise

Ninety thousand miles up to the blue skies.

If the wind slows down and inclines to stop,

It'll turn the sea upside down with a flop.

The world may regard my talk as so queer;

Hearing me like that, at my words they jeer.

Teacher said a child may strike one with awe;

One should never a little child ignore!

* roc: in Arabian and Persian legend, an enormous and powerful bird of prey. According to *Sir Lush*, the giant bird is a symbol of universal force or the operation of such a force, as reads like this: There in North Sea is a fish called Minnow, whose body spans about a thousand miles. When transformed into a bird, it is called Roc, whose back spans about a thousand miles.
* Yung Li: Yung Li (A.D. 678 - A.D. 747), a famous poet and calligrapher, and an outspoken official, killed later by Premier Linfu Li out of schemes and intrigues.

* Teacher: referring to Confucius, who had 72 outstanding disciples out of several thousand students, extolled as a teacher of all by emperors, scholars and the general population in later generations.

赠张公洲革处士

抱瓮灌秋蔬，
心闲游天云。
每将瓜田叟，
耕种汉水濆。
时登张公洲，
入兽不乱群。
井无枯槔事，
门绝刺绣文。
长揖二千石，
远辞百里君。
斯为真隐者，
吾党慕清芬。

To Ke, a Clerk from Chang's Shoal

You water the greens with an urn,
Your heart with drifting clouds does turn.
You call yourself a melon man,
Living and tilling by the Han.
You are from Chang's Shoal, so says one;
When you go to herds, they don't run.
You do not with craft fish for fame;
Extravagance is not your aim.
Prefects you simply nod to greet,
And magistrates you will not meet.
A hermit you are, high and higher;

Your holiness I do admire.

* the Han: the Han River, the longest branch of the Long River, having an important position in Chinese history.
* Chang's Shoal: a shoal about 5 kilometers from Mightboom, i.e. today's Wuchang, Wuhan, Hupei Province.
* melon: a trailing plant of the gourd family, or its fruit. There are two genera, the muskmelon and the watermelon, each with numerous varieties, growing in both tropical and temperate zones.

古近体诗二十四首
Old-new Rhythmic Poetry, 24 Poems

秋日炼药院镊白发，赠元六兄林宗

木落识岁秋，
瓶冰知天寒。
桂枝日已绿，
拂雪凌云端。
弱龄接光景，
矫翼攀鸿鸾。
投分三十载，
荣枯同所欢。
长吁望青云，
镊白坐相看。
秋颜入晓镜，
壮发凋危冠。
穷与鲍生贾，
饥从漂母餐。
时来极大人，
道在岂吟叹。
乐毅方适赵，
苏秦初说韩。
卷舒固在我，
何事空摧残。

To Lintsung Yüan Six, Sighing o'er Gray Hair at Concoction Yard on an Autumn Day

It's autumn as leaves fall from trees;

It's winter since water does freeze.
A laurel turns green day by day
And sweeps snowy clouds with its spray.
A young man tries to grasp a breeze;
A fledgling will outrun wild geese.
We have been friends for thirty years,
Sharing gains and pains, cheers and fears.
We look at the clouds in despair
And sitting, sigh o'er our gray hair.
My wrinkles mirrored I look at;
My hair feels thin in my loose hat.
Poor, we barter for livelihood
And we beg from Washer for food.
Our chance may fall out of the sky;
With the Word, why heave a long sigh?
Like how Ee Yüeh to Chao had fled;
Like how Ch'in Su to Han had said.
We do things or not for our joy;
Then, why should we ourselves destroy?

* laurel: laurus nobilis, an evergreen shrub with aromatic, lance-shaped leaves, yellowish flowers, and succulent, cherry-like fruit, a symbol of glory usually in the form of a crown or wreath of laurel to indicate honor or high merit, especially when one had passed Grand Test in ancient China. In Chinese mythology, there is a laurel tree on the moon, and it would never fall even though Kang Wu has kept cutting it.
* wild goose: an undomesticated goose that is caring and responsible, taken as a symbol of benevolence, righteousness, good manner, wisdom, and faith in Chinese culture.
* Washer: referring to Washing Mother who provided Hsin Han with food when the later commander was poor.
* the Word: referring to Tao if transliterated, the most significant and profoundest concept in Chinese philosophy. The Word is identifiable with the Word or Logos in the West, as there is an enormous amount of common ground in the two cosmologies and the doctrines concerning the most fundamental matters such as "the Word is the One"

and "God is the One", and the personalization of Being, the progenitor of finite spirits, which are subordinate kinds of Beingor merely appearances of the Divine, the One.

* Ee Yüeh: a prominent military commander. In the year of 284 B.C., he commanded the five-nation allied forces to attack the State of Ch'i and set an example of the weak overcoming the strong in war history.
* Ch'in Su (? - 284 B.C.): a political strategist in the Warring States period. When he succeeded, it occurred to him that if he had a farmland at early age, he would not have been a prime minister. When young, he went out, seeking for a career, but returned in rags and tatters. His wife would not take the trouble of leaving her place at the loom to greet him. However, he succeeded later in his scheme of the federation of six weaker states against the strong state of Ch'in, and he was appointed prime minister of each of the six states thus combined.

书情赠蔡舍人雄

尝高谢太傅，
携妓东山门。
楚舞醉碧云，
吴歌断清猿。
暂因苍生起，
谈笑安黎元。
余亦爱此人，
丹霄冀飞翻。
遭逢圣明主，
敢进兴亡言。
白璧竟何辜？
青蝇遂成冤。
一朝去京国，
十载客梁园。
猛犬吠九关，
杀人愤精魂。
皇穹雪冤枉，
白日开氛昏。
太阶得夔龙，
桃李满中原。
倒海索明月，
凌山采芳荪。
愧无横草功，
虚负雨露恩。
迹谢云台阁，
心随天马辕。
夫子王佐才，

而今复谁论?
层飙振六翮,
不日思腾骞。
我纵五湖棹,
烟涛恣崩奔。
梦钓子陵湍,
英风缅犹存。
徒希客星隐,
弱植不足援。
千里一回首,
万里一长歌。
黄鹤不复来,
清风奈愁何!
舟浮潇湘月,
山倒洞庭波。
投汨笑古人,
临濠得天和。
闲时田亩中,
搔背牧鸡鹅。
别离解相访,
应在武陵多。

To Secretary Man Tsai

I admired An Hsieh very well;
In the East Hills, he held a belle.
Her dance did the white clouds entice;
Her song did the monkey's cries slice.
His efforts did the folks sustain;
His laughter did them entertain.

Such a person I do adore;
One day to the sky I may soar.
Today at His Majesty's call,
I dare talk about rise and fall.
If white jade is stained with the shit
Of a fly, must the jade bear it?
Once I am forced to leave the court,
For ten years to Liang I'll resort.
Ferocious dogs at just ones bark;
The wronged spirits rage in the dark.
The Lord all evils does erase,
Like the sun sweeping off the haze.
Brilliant sages He does obtain,
With all talents in the Mid-plain.
From the oceans bright pearls are got;
In the mountains sweet sedge is sought.
What a shame, little have I done,
Having had much shine from the sun.
Tho from Heaven Mound I'm apart,
My heart follows His sedan cart.
You are His Majesty's great beam,
But who does hold you in esteem?
Now you flutter your wings to rise;
Soon you will get close to the skies.
I'll just in Five Lakes row my boat,
Upon the misty waves afloat.
I dreamed of Sir Hill last night,
His virtue decors hills with light.
I admire Sir Hill all in vain;
So feeble, who could I sustain?
Having gone so far, I turn back

And to Long Peace I sing, alack.

The yellow crane will not back fly;

To the chill wind I can but sigh.

Boats on the Hsiang, the moonlit chill;

Waves of Cavehall, the fallen hill.

I laugh at the man drowned in vain;

I admire Lush who swam to gain.

I will farm, enjoying a breeze,

And scratch my back while herding geese.

If one day you want to find me,

In Fairyland there I must be.

* An Hsieh: An Hsieh (A.D. 320 – A.D. 385), a general, statesman and renowned scholar in the Eastern Chin dynasty. An Hsieh, with this love for his country life as well as for scholarship, but going to the service of the nation in time of need, was the favourite Chinese type of hero in ancient China.
* the East Hills: located in today's Shaohsing, Chechiang Province, a place for reclusion, where An Hsieh (A.D. 320 – A.D. 385), a general and scholar, used to live.
* fly: one of various small dipterous insects (family *Muscidae*), especially the common housefly. The fly, especially the bluebottle, is a nasty slanderer in Chinese culture, like a section of a verse from *The Book of Songs* reads: "Upon the hazels o'er there, / Alight the buzzing flies. / Those mean men you trust ne'er, / They estrange us with lies."
* dog: a domesticated carnivorous mammal (*Canis familiaris*), of worldwide distribution and many varieties, noted for its adaptability and its devotion to man.
* sedge: a grasslike cyperaceous herb with flowers densely clustered in spikes; widely distributed in marshy places.
* the Five Lakes: referring to Lake T'ai and the other four lakes around. As legend goes, Li Fan (536 B.C.– 448 B.C.), a renowned statesman, strategist, economist and Wordist in the Spring and Autumn period, changed his name to live in seclusion among the Five Lakes after he helped the State of Yüeh wipe out Wu.
* Sir Hill: Tzuling Yan (39 B.C.– A.D. 41) if transliterated, a renowned hermit in the Han dynasty. He showed his talent at an early age. After Hsiu Liu was enthroned to be the emperor of Han, Hill was invited several times to serve the court. Though the

emperor was an acquaintance of his, Yan declined the offer and chose to live in seclusion in the Richspring Hills.

* the man drowned in vain: referring to Yüan Ch'ü (340 B.C.- 278 B.C.), a great patriotic poet and official of Ch'u, who threw himself into a river, so aggrieved at his broken state.
* Cavehall: referring to Lake Cavehall, a lake in Hunan Province.
* Lush: Sir Lush (369 B.C.- 286 B.C.), a great thinker, philosopher and litterateur in the Warring States Period. As a principal founder of Wordism, Sir Lush enjoys a high reputation, the same as Laocius.

忆襄阳旧游赠马少府巨

昔为大堤客，
曾上山公楼。
开窗碧嶂满，
拂镜沧江流。
高冠佩雄剑，
长揖韩荆州。
此地别夫子，
今来思旧游。
朱颜君未老，
白发我先秋。
壮志恐蹉跎，
功名若云浮。
归心结远梦，
落日悬春愁。
空思羊叔子，
堕泪岘山头。

To Chü Ma, My Old Friend in Sowshine, a County Sheriff

I once toured the dike by the town
And from Hermit's Tower I looked down.
The green hills set my window green;
The blue rill makes my mirror sheen.
With my sword, wearing a high crown,
I bowed to Han, head of Chaste Town.

I took leave of you here that year;
To see you again I'm back here.
Good health you enjoy, young as e'er,
But I have grown old with gray hair.
How time flies and nothing will stay!
Ranks and fame like clouds drift away.
My dream is there; back home I'll go!
The setting sun stirs up my woe.
Missing Sir Goat, I'm in thought deep;
Tears brimming, I look at Mt. Steep.

* Hermit's Tower: the hermit Hillman's tower built when Hillman was Prefect of Sowshine.
* Chaste Town: Chasteton, Chingchow if transliterated, an important city on the Long River, in today's Hupei Province.
* Sir Goat: or Lord Goat, a commander in the Chin dynasty, who garrisoned in Sowshine. He promoted schooling and won over the trust of the people and the soldiers with nobility. To memorize his achievements, the people in Sowshine set a tablet on Mt. Steep. As the people could not help shedding tears once they saw the tablet, they named it Tablet Tear.
* Mt. Steep: an important fort in history, located in the southwest of Sowshine (Hsiangyang), the River Han to its east.

对雪献从兄虞城宰

昨夜梁园里，
弟寒兄不知。
庭前看玉树，
肠断忆连枝。

To My Cousin, Mayor of Yü, a Verse Written in Snow

I stayed in Prince Liang's Park last night;
Me cold, you did not know my plight.
In the court, viewing trees in snow,
I thought of twin trees, drowned in woe.

* Yü: a major city in the Hsia dynasty, that is, today's Yü County, Honan Province. In the early Hsia dynasty, the place was enfeoffed by Worm to Hibiscus's son, which was later known as the State of Yü. When Hotspring (cir. 1670 B.C.- 1587 B.C.) founded Shang after having exterminated Hsia (cir. 21 B.C.- 16 B.C.), he made this place his capital.
* Prince Liang's Park: a royal park established by Prince Piety of Liang in the Western Han dynasty, built on the ruins of the State of Sung, that is, today's Shangch'iu, Honan Province, the birthplace of Sir Lush, one of the forerunners of Wordism.

访道安陵遇盖还为余造真箓,临别留赠

清水见白石,
仙人识青童。
安陵盖夫子,
十岁与天通。
悬河与微言,
谈论安可穷。
能令二千石,
抚背惊神聪。
挥毫赠新诗,
高价掩山东。
至今平原客,
感激慕清风。
学道北海仙,
传书蕊珠宫。
丹田了玉阙,
白日思云空。
为我草真箓,
天人惭妙工。
七元洞豁落,
八角辉星虹。
三灾荡璇玑,
蛟龙翼微躬。
举手谢天地,
虚无齐始终。
黄金满高堂,
答荷难克充。
下笑世上士,

沉魂北罗酆。
昔日万乘坟，
今成一科蓬。
赠言若可重，
实此轻华嵩。

To Huan Kai Who, Made a Wordist Figure for Me in Peaceridge

Clear water does white pebbles show;
An immortal does a child know.
Teacher Kai who's from Peaceridge, then
Could commune with Heaven at ten.
He could talk of what is profound,
Reaching far away, without bound.
The prefect could be so amazed
That he stroked the child who was graced.
With your brush you wrote a verse nice,
In Shantung ranked the highest price.
E'en hangers-on of Chao today
Admire your virtue and your way.
You learn the Word at North Sea there;
And in Pistil you teach skills rare.
White air from your navel does rise
And at daytime you muse the skies.
Your work gives the fairy a start;
She feels shy with your greatest art.
How smart and fluent the strokes are
While sparkling like Octagon Star.
The Big Dipper sweeps off banes rife;

> The dragon brings back a new life.
> Hands raised to thank Heaven and earth;
> You'll last with them in length and girth.
> Gems and gold piled up in the hall
> Cannot repay your grace at all.
> How funny, humans in the world,
> To Hades below you'll be hurled.
> The emperors' high tombs of yore
> Are rampant with grass, seen no more.
> My words to you now, full of power,
> Outweigh Mt. Flora and Mt. Tower.

* Peaceridge: a county in Hopei See (an administrative area mainly in today's Hopei Province) in the T'ang dynasty.
* brush: any of various writing brushes or called Chinese brush, widely used for writing or painting, invented or renovated by Tien Meng (259 B.C.- 210 B.C.), a general in the Ch'in dynasty.
* hangers-on of Chao: referring to the hangers-on of Lord Plain of Chao. Lord Plain was one of the Four Childes in the Warring States period.
* the Word: referring to Tao if transliterated, the most significant and profoundest concept in Chinese philosophy. According to Laocius's *The Word and the World*: "The Word is void, but its use is infinite. O deep! It seems to be the root of all things." The Word is identifiable with the Word or Logos in the West, as there is an enormous amount of common ground in the two cosmologies and doctrines concerning the most fundamental matters of creation and human nature.
* North Sea: what is today's Ch'ingchow, Shantung Province.
* Pistil: a fairy palace in Wordist myths.
* Octagon Star: probably referring to the Word or the profundity of the Word.
* the Big Dipper: the Dipper, a constellation composed of seven bright stars, which looks like a spoon in the sky.
* dragon: a fabulous serpent-like giant winged animal that can change its girth and length, a totem of the Chinese nation, a symbol of benevolence and sovereignty in Chinese culture.

* Mt. Flora: one of the Five Sacred Mountains in China, located in Shanhsi Province.
* Mt. Tower: located in the west of present-day Honan Province, one of the Five Mountains esteemed highly in Chinese culture.

赠崔郎中宗之

胡雁拂海翼,
翱翔鸣素秋。
惊云辞沙朔,
飘荡迷河洲。
有如飞蓬人,
去逐万里游。
登高望浮云,
仿佛如旧丘。
日从海旁没,
水向天边流。
长啸倚孤剑,
目极心悠悠。
岁晏归去来,
富贵安可求。
仲尼七十说,
历聘莫见收。
鲁连逃千金,
圭组岂可酬。
时哉苟不会,
草木为我俦。
希君同携手,
长往南山幽。

To Secretary Tsungchih Ts'ui

The north wild geese to the sea shrill,

While soaring through the autumn chill.
The startled clouds drift from the sand
And to rivers and shoals expand.
The vagrants drift like thistledown
For ten thousand miles from the town.
Climbing high and seeing clouds roam,
I feel them like the knolls at home.
By seashore the setting sun glows;
To the skyline the river flows.
Leaning on my sword I long shout;
My eyesight far away goes out.
This year is gone away, no more,
Ranks and riches where to look for?
Confucius, seventy years old,
None of his teachings could be sold.
Chunglien was offered a good pay;
From all offers he went away.
If right time does not come to me,
With plants and grass I want to be.
With you I would go side by side,
And in the South Hills we'd long bide.

* wild goose: an undomesticated goose that is caring and responsible, taken as a symbol of benevolence, righteousness, good manner, wisdom, and faith in Chinese culture.
* Confucius: Confucius (551 B.C.- 479 B.C.), a renowned thinker, educator and statesman in the Spring and Autumn period, born in the State of Lu, who was the founder of Confucianism and who had exerted profound influence on Chinese culture. He is one of the few leaders who based their philosophy on the virtues that are required for the day-to-day living. His philosophy centered on personal and governmental morality, correctness of social relationships, justice and sincerity.
* Chunglien: Chunglien Lu (305 B.C.- 245 B.C.), a sophist from Ch'i in the late Spring and Autumn period. He declined to be titled and awarded by Lord Plain of Chao, and left for East Sea.

赠崔咨议

绿骥本天马,
素非伏枥驹。
长嘶向清风,
倏忽凌九区。
何言西北至,
却走东南隅?
世道有翻覆,
前期难豫图。
希君一剪拂,
犹可骋中衢。

To Ts'ui, a Consultant

Green Steed is a horse aiming high,
Not a pony with its manger by.
To the high wind, with a loud neigh,
It gallops through the land, no stay.
Why do you come here from northwest
And go southeast without a rest?
The world can be turned off the land;
Nothing can be planned before hand.
Please, sir, give me some of your care,
I could run on the thoroughfare!

---

* Green Steed: one of the Eight Horses of King Solemn of Chough.
* horse: a large solid-hoofed quadruped (*Equus caballus*) with coarse mane and tail, of

various strains: Ferghana, Mongolian, Kazaks, Hequ, Karasahr and so on and of various colors: black, white, yellow, brown, dappled and so on, commonly in the domesticated state, employed as a beast of draught and burden and especially for riding upon.

赠昇州王使君忠臣

六代帝王国，
三吴佳丽城。
贤人当重寄，
天子借高名。
巨海一边静，
长江万里清。
应须救赵策，
未肯弃侯嬴。

To Loyal Wang, a Civil Governor of Sunrise

For six dynasties, Place of Crown,
It's a beautiful southern town.
Sages are put to full use here;
Sons of Heaven your name revere.
The ocean by you keeps serene;
The Yangtze River long is clean.
You have plans to save the Chao State;
Don't forget Ying who kept the gate.

* Sunrise: a state in the T'ang dynasty, whose prefecture office was located in present-day Nanking.
* Sons of Heaven: kings or emperors, who have divine kinship.
* the Yangtze River: the lower reaches of the Long River, from Nanking to the estuary.
* The Chao State: the State of Chao (403 B.C.- 222 B.C.), a vassal state in the Spring

and Autumn period, one of the Seven Powers in the Warring States period.
* Ying: referring to Ying Hou (? – 257 B.C.), a hermit living as a porter of Smooth Gate of the State of Way and became a hanger-one of Prince Faithridge.

赠别从甥高五

鱼目高泰山，
不如一玙璠。
贤甥即明月，
声价动天门。
能成吾宅相，
不减魏阳元。
自顾寡筹略，
功名安所存？
五木思一掷，
如绳系穷猿。
枥中骏马空，
堂上醉人喧。
黄金久已罄，
为报故交恩。
闻君陇西行，
使我惊心魂。
与尔共飘飖，
云天各飞翻。
江水流或卷，
此心难具论。
贫家羞好客，
语拙觉辞繁。
三朝空错莫，
对饭却惭冤。
自笑我非夫，
生事多契阔。
蓄积万古愤，

向谁得开豁？
天地一浮云，
此身乃毫末。
忽见无端倪，
太虚可包括。
去去何足道，
临歧空复愁。
肝胆不楚越，
山河亦衾裯。
云龙若相从，
明主会见收。
成功解相访，
溪水桃花流。

Farewell to Kao Five, My Nephew

Fish eyes piled as high as Mt. Tower
Cannot compare with jadeite dower.
Nephew, you are a pearl so great,
More valuable than Heaven's Gate.
You'll be a premier in our tree;
Compared with you Yang Wei can't be.
Look at me, with no plans or aim,
However could I come to fame?
Five dice I would throw with all might;
I'm like a monkey tethered tight!
From the manger the horse is gone;
In the hall the drunkards wild run.
I have now spent all of my gold
To repay my friends young and old.

You're going to West Bulge I hear;
I'm so shaken, surprised with fear.
Drifting and drifting, you and I
Would go apart under the sky.
A river flowing may be bent;
My sadness I can hardly vent.
A poor host as a shy host goes;
A slow tongue hates to be verbose.
We have wasted time for three days;
Before the meals, I'm shamed, no ways.
I sneer at myself I've no gains;
My life is filled up with all pains.
The age-old gloom pent up in me,
Who could get it and set me free?
Heaven or earth is but a flip,
And I'm just like a tiny tip.
It revolves on, a boundless ball;
The cosmos can contain it all.
Farther and farther while we go,
We come to crossroads, full of rue.
We are close by, not far away;
You there, me here, so near we stay.
When right time comes to you and me,
The Lord will employ us with glee.
Well done, you may come for a chat;
My creek flows with blossoms like that.

* fish eye: a metaphor for something cheap or fake. It is said that a man bought a big pearl and his neighbor was jealous. On one occasion, the neighbor found a big fish eye and trumpeted he had a pearl.
* Mt. Tower: located in the west of present-day Honan Province, one of the Five Sacred

Mountains, highly honored in Chinese culture.
* pearl: a smooth, lustrous, usually white and bluish-gray, calcareous concretion deposited in layers around a central nucleus in the shells of various mollusks or oysters, and largely used as a gem, medicine or given as a gift, a metaphor for the dearest one, a representation of nobility, purity and dignity in Chinese culture.
* Yang Wei: Yang Wei (A.D. 209 - A.D. 290), referring to a minister with high reputation in the Way and Chin dynasties. A fortuneteller once told his uncle that there would be a renowned nephew coming from the house, which implied that Wei would make remarkable achievements in the future.
* West Bulge: Lunghsi if transliterated, name of a shire in the Warring States period and the T'ang dynasty, located in the southeast of present-day Kansu Province, covering Lanchow, West Buldge and Lint'ao. It has been a strategic vantage point since ancient times and has left us a rich legacy of Yangshao Culture and the Chi's culture.
* cosmos: the world or universe considered as a system, perfect in order and arrangement, opposed to chaos.

赠裴司马

翡翠黄金缕,
绣成歌舞衣。
若无云间月,
谁可比光辉。
秀色一如此,
多为众女讥。
君恩移昔爱,
失宠秋风归。
愁苦不窥邻,
泣上流黄机。
天寒素手冷,
夜长烛复微。
十日不满匹,
鬓蓬乱若丝。
犹是可怜人,
容华世中稀。
向君发皓齿,
顾我莫相违。

To Commander P'ei

With jadeite and gold thread bright,
A dancing dress is made, so light.
Save the moon that mid clouds does glare,
Who else can with your charm compare?
Your elegance that all eyes steers

Incurs so many ladies' jeers.
The Lord, charmed no more, moves thither;
Not favored, in chills you wither.
Behold, those ladies drowned in gloom
Sprinkle their tears to the brown loom.
The coldness freezes their hands slight;
Night long, dim is the candlelight.
They can't finish a roll for ten days;
The dishevelled hair sadly sways.
They are ladies lovely and fair;
In this world they're something so rare.
Showing off teeth pearled, they smile:
Do not miss your chance, the best while.

* the moon: the planet of the earth, which appears at night and gives off shining silvery light, an image of purity and solitude in Chinese culture.
* Showing glistening teeth, they smile: an allusion to Chih Ts'ao's line: Who speaks for her betwixt teeth pearled?

叙旧赠江阳宰陆调

太伯让天下,
仲雍扬波涛。
清风荡万古,
迹与星辰高。
开吴食东溟,
陆氏世英髦。
夫子特峻秀,
岳立冠人曹。
风流少年时,
京洛事游遨。
腰间延陵剑,
玉剑明珠袍。
我昔斗鸡徒,
连延五陵豪。
邀遮相组织,
呵吓来煎熬。
君开万丛人,
鞍马皆辟易。
告急清宪台,
脱余北门厄。
间宰江阳邑,
翦棘树兰芳。
城门何肃穆,
五月飞秋霜。
好鸟集珍木,
高才列华堂。
时从府中归,

丝管俨成行。
但苦隔远道,
无由共衔觞。
江北荷花开,
江南杨梅熟。
正好饮酒时,
怀贤在心目。
挂席拾海月,
乘风下长川。
多沽新丰醑,
满载剡溪船。
中途不遇人,
直到尔门前。
大笑同一醉,
取乐平生年。

To T'iao Lu, Magistrate of Rivershine, Talking about the Old Days

Greatone declined the demised throne;
Usetwo founded his state alone.
How great their values and gains are!
Their merits can outshine a star.
The Suns established Eastern Wu;
The Lus did offer heroes true.
Teacher, like a peak you stand tall,
Your talents overpowering all.
When I was a dude, a young man;
I toured in the capital then.
A Broadridge sword hung on my waist,

A belt jeweled and a gown laced.
With the cock fighters I once fought;
From Pentaridge rascals they brought.
All hooligans they seemed to be,
Who tried to lord it over me.
At that time you rushed thru the crowd
And shooed away the steeds aloud.
You reported to the policemen,
So I was saved at North Gate then.
Of Rivershine you're magistrate,
Crashing the bad, rearing the great.
So grave looks the gate of the town,
Like frost in the fifth moon falls down.
As good birds gather in trees tall;
So talents crowd in your grand hall.
You come back from office to dine
While the lutes and flutes form a line.
Now from you I am far away,
I can't drink with you for a day.
North, the lotuses are in bloom;
South, the plums ripe and balm your room.
To drink, the best hours I can find;
Your grace I keep fast in my mind.
Now to the sea I set my sail
And go downstream there with a hail.
I buy Newrich wine and buy more;
A boat with a full load I oar.
On the way here, I'll see no one;
So I can reach your door anon!
I will drink a cup to your smile;
Why don't we play every while?

* Rivershine: a county in Yangchow, Huainan See in the T'ang dynasty.
* Greatone: referring to the eldest son of Father Verity of Chough, also styled Sonone. Sonone and his brother Sontwo moved to the east to decline the throne, and established the State of Wu.
* Usetwo: referring to the second son of Father Verity of Chough, also styled Sontwo. He moved to the east with his elder brother Greatone to leave the throne to Throughfour, his younger brother.
* the Suns: referring to the House of Sun who established Eastern Wu in the Three Kingdoms period. Chien Sun (A.D. 155 – A.D. 191) and Ts'e Sun (A.D. 175 – A.D. 200) laid the foundation for latter achievements, and Ch'üan Sun (A.D. 182 – A.D. 252), Great Emperor, established Eastern Wu, a self-claimed empire.
* the Lus: referring to a powerful clan serving the Suns in the Three Kingdoms period.
* Broadridge: a land of Wu in the Spring and Autumn period, belonging to Stripfour (576 B.C.– 484 B.C.), who declined the throne and farmed in Broadridge.
* Broadridge sword: When Stripfour (576 B.C.– 484 B.C.), Chi Cha if transliterated, or styled Sir Four of Broadridge, traveled to State of Hsu, the king liked his sword but was reluctant to ask for it. Stripfour did not give the sword because his journey had not been finished. When Stripfour came back, he found the lord had already passed away, so Stripfour left his sword at the tomb of the king as a gift.
* Pentaridge: referring to the area where the tombs of five emperors of Han are located. In the Han and T'ang dynasties, Pentaridge implied a residential area of rich people.
* lotus: a plant of the waterlily family, noted for their large leaves floating on water and showy red or white flowers, a symbol of purity and elegance in Chinese culture, unsoiled though out of soil, so clean with all leaves green.
* plum: a kind of plant or the edible purple drupaceous fruit of the plant which is any one of various trees of the genus *Prunus*.
* Newrich: a county, built by Pang Liu in imitation of his hometown Rich County, in today's Lintung County, Sha'anhsi Province, famous for its wine, the best wine in the T'ang dynasty.

赠从孙义兴宰铭

天子思茂宰,
天枝得英才。
朗然清秋月,
独出映吴台。
落笔生绮绣,
操刀振风雷。
蠖屈虽百里,
鹏骞望三台。
退食无外事,
琴堂向山开。
绿水寂以闲,
白云有时来。
河阳富奇藻,
彭泽纵名杯。
所恨不见之,
犹如仰昭回。
元恶昔滔天,
疲人散幽草。
惊川无活鳞,
举邑罕遗老。
誓雪会稽耻,
将奔宛陵道。
亚相素所重,
投刃应桑林。
独坐伤激扬,
神融一开襟。
弦歌欣再理,

和乐醉人心。
蠹政除害马，
倾巢有归禽。
壶浆候君来，
聚舞共讴吟。
农人弃蓑笠，
蚕女堕缨簪。
欢笑相拜贺，
则知惠爱深。
历职吾所闻，
称贤尔为最。
化洽一邦上，
名驰三江外。
峻节贯云霄，
通方堪远大。
能文变风俗，
好客留轩盖。
他日一来游，
因之严光濑。

To My Grandnephew, Ming Li, Magistrate of Rightrise

The Lord needs a good magistrate,
Hence you, an official so great.
You, so young, in the moonlight drowned,
Send forth bright beams to the Wu Mound.
You write articles magnificent,
So capable, so efficient!
Tho it's thirty-miles, inchworm size,

A roc, to Triune Dais you'll rise.
Office hours finished, you are free;
In Lute Hall facing hills you'll be.
Now free, the water green you play;
Betimes the white clouds come to stay.
Pan Yüeh's brilliance you may outshine;
With Ch'ien T'ao you can vie for wine.
You could not see them any way,
Though in different places you stay.
Some felons are heinous, alas;
The tired folks are dispersed in grass.
Frightened rivers no live fish hold;
The county sees few people old.
Mt. Summit Shame I will revenge;
I'm on my way to Winding Range.
You have your superiors' respect;
You handle affairs with effect.
Sitting alone, sometimes inspired,
You can have your results desired.
And then you pluck the lute with glee
So intoxicating, so free.
You have the criminals pressed down;
All folks go back to their hometown.
They entertain you with good food;
Then you dance in a happy mood.
The farmers their cape and hat fling;
The girls, hairpin off, dance and sing.
They laugh with glee and celebrate
Their boon and your favor so great.
Of all magistrates I have seen;
You are the best: best you have been.

You nurture a county, a town,
And your fame has far away flown.
Your character rings to the skies;
You well know the wherefores and whys.
Your articles change the folks' way;
Your smiles invite people to stay.
One day, I will again come here,
Because there's someone we revere.

* Triune Dais: referring to a constellation in Chinese astrology or to the official system in the T'ang dynasty, which includes Privy Council (Central Secretariat Department), Censorate (Undergate Department) and Executive (Administration Department).
* Lute Hall: a magistrate's residence.
* Yüeh Pan: Yüeh Pan (A.D. 247 – A.D. 300), referring to An Pan, a renowned litterateur in the Western Chin dynasty.
* Ch'ien T'ao: referring to Poolbright T'ao (A.D. 352 – A.D. 427), a verse writer, poet, and litterateur in the Chin dynasty, the founder of Chinese idyllism, and once the magistrate of P'engtse.
* Mt. Summit: the K'uaichi Mountains in present-day Chechiang Province, where Worm convened a summit attended by vassal lords, hence the name.
* Winding Range: a birthplace of Chinese Literature located in present-day Anhui, abounding with cultural and historic attractions such as Mt. Chingt'ting.
* someone we revere: referring to Sir Yanridge, a renowned hermit in the Eastern Han dynasty.

草创大还赠柳官迪

天地为橐籥，
周流行太易。
造化合元符，
交媾腾精魄。
自然成妙用，
孰知其指的。
罗络四季间，
绵微无一隙。
日月更出没，
双光岂云只？
姹女乘河车，
黄金充辕轭。
执枢相管辖，
摧伏伤羽翮。
朱鸟张炎威，
白虎守本宅。
相煎成苦老，
消铄凝津液。
仿佛明窗尘，
死灰同至寂。
捣冶入赤色，
十二周律历。
赫然称大还，
与道本无隔。
白日可抚弄，
清都在咫尺。
北酆落死名，

南斗上生籍。
抑予是何者，
身在方士格。
才术信纵横，
世途自轻掷。
吾求仙弃俗，
君晓损胜益。
不向金阙游，
思为玉皇客。
鸾车速风电，
龙骑无鞭策。
一举上九天，
相携同所适。

To Kuanti Liu upon the First Concoction of Gold Pills

Bellows-like are Heaven and earth,
From the chaos to the great worth.
Shade and Shine in combination,
Spirits run for copulation.
The way of nature is so fine;
All should know the meaning of Sign.
It turns from season to season,
So smooth, such a great diapason.
Sun and moon, not early or late,
Day by day, routinely alternate.
Mercury rides in River Cart;
Three carts of gold for her will start.
The pivot should be held with care,

Lest one hurt fledglings in the air.
Peacocks like to show off their power;
Tigers crawl down to hide their dower.
Cold and heat is mixed so to kill;
Slobber is saved for a life pill.
A heart is live dust on the sill;
Only dead ash can remain still.
Red grit is blended to pestle,
To turn from cycle to cycle.
Therefore, gold pills are made anon;
With the Word they are really one.
One can play the sun in the sky,
The celestial castle nearby.
Death, from the Dipper go away!
Life, near Sagittarius do stay!
Who is Pai Li, o who is me?
A necromancer I must be!
With my craft I travel the sky;
All worldly ways I would deny.
I would go to find my pure fay;
You know the secrets of the way.
The gold palaces we will flee;
With Jade Emperor we will be.
The phoenix cart runs like a whir;
The best horse you don't need to spur.
Let's soar high across the ninth sky
And to Fairyland there we fly.

---

* Shade and Shine: the most important and basic concept of Chinese or Eastern philosophy, characterized by three features: identification, opposition and interconversion, although apparently standing for two poles of binary opposition.

* River Cart: a term in Chinese alchemy. Since the T'ang dynasty, there have been two explanations of River Cart: firstly, it refers to kidneys; secondly, vapour that circulates endlessly.
* peacock: the male of a gallinaceous crested bird (genus *Pavo*), which has the tail coverts enormously elongated, erectile, and marked with ocelli or eyelike spots and the neck and breast of an irridescent greenish blue.
* tiger: a large carnivorous feline mammal of Asia, with vertical black wavy stripes on a tawny body and black bars or rings on the limbs and tail, praised as king of all animals.
* the Word: referring to Tao if transliterated, the most significant and profoundest concept in Chinese philosophy. According to Laocius's *The Word and the World*: "The Word is void, but its use is infinite. O deep! It seems to be the root of all things."
* the Dipper: a constellation composed of seven bright stars.
* Sagittarius: a Zodiacal constellation, pictured as Centaur shooting an arrow; the Archer.
* Jade Emperor: formally called Celestial Supreme Utmost Natural Wonderful Encompassing Truest Jade Emperor at Gold Gate, the deity with highest power in Chinese mythology and Wordist literature.
* the Ninth Sky: the vast empyrean, the highest of Heavens, the highest of the nine layers of the sky according to Chinese legend, and a similar notion in Dante's *Divina Commedia* in the west, *The Lüs' Spring and Autumn* in China and Buddhist Sutras from India.
* Fairyland: an imaginary ideal abode for immortals, sometimes thought of as being in the middle of East Sea, sometimes high above in the sky, as is this poem.

赠崔司户文昆季

双珠出海底,
俱是连城珍。
明月两特达,
馀辉傍照人。
英声振名都,
高价动殊邻。
岂伊箕山故,
特以风期亲。
惟昔不自媒,
担簦西入秦。
攀龙九天上,
忝列岁星臣。
布衣侍丹墀,
密勿草丝纶。
才微惠渥重,
谗巧生缁磷。
一去已十载,
今来复盈旬。
清霜入晓鬓,
白露生衣巾。
侧见绿水亭,
开门列华茵。
千金散义士,
四坐无凡宾。
欲折月中桂,
持为寒者薪。
路傍已窃笑,

天路将何因？
垂恩倘丘山，
报德有微身。

To Wenk'un Ts'ui, a Household Registrar

The two pearls in the sea you find,
More precious than two towns combined.
The twin bright moons if you expose,
They shine all with remanent glows.
Their name through Capital glistens,
Their price the neighborhoods frightens.
Is it because you're from Dustpan
That you are an enticing man?
As a friend did me recommend,
With a sunshade I did west wend.
So I could see the Lord divine,
Joining in the ministers' line.
A low man on the red steps bright
Did wait there for edicts to write.
With His grace, I was a good one;
So slandered, I lost my shine anon.
Since then ten years has gone away;
And now it's been a ten-day stay.
Frost has touched my hair with its white;
Dew has soaked my clothes to shine bright.
The pavilion sees water sheen;
The door beholds a carpet green.
I'll spend all gold on a good treat,

Because all my friends here are great.
I'd pluck laurel sprays from the moon;
I'll give them to friends for their boon.
A passer-by at me does jeer:
By what means can you go up there?
If one can give me a small knoll,
I will repay him with my whole.

* pearl: a lustrous, calcareous concretion deposited in layers around a central nucleus in the shells of various mollusks, and largely used as a gem.
* Dustpan: a place in present-day Shantung Province. It's said that Mound visited Freedom (Yu Hsu) at Dustpan and intended to abdicate the throne to him. Hsu felt that he did not deserve it, however, and retreated to a farming life at Dustpan.
* red steps: the steps, painted in red, leading up to an imperial palace or an official or monastic hall, frequently occurring in classic Chinese literature.
* edict: a public ordinance emanating from a sovereign and having the force of law.
* carp: fresh water food fish (*Ciprinus carpiao*), common in China, a mascot in Chinese culture, symbolizing great success and harmony. A popular idiom "a carp jumping over the Dragon Gate" means climbing up the social ladder or succeeding in the imperial civil service examination.
* laurel sprays from the moon: In Chinese mythology, there is a Laurel tree on the moon, and it would never fall even though Kang Wu, a banished immortal, kept cutting it.

赠溧阳宋少府陟

李斯未相秦,
且逐东门兔。
宋玉事襄王,
能为高唐赋。
常闻绿水曲,
忽此相逢遇。
扫洒青天开,
豁然披云雾。
葳蕤紫鸾鸟,
巢在昆山树。
惊风西北吹,
飞落南溟去。
早怀经济策,
特受龙颜顾。
白玉栖青蝇,
君臣忽行路。
人生感分义,
贵欲呈丹素。
何日清中原,
相期廓天步。

To Chih Sung, Sheriff of Lishine

Before Ssu Li served Ch'in, the great,
He chased rabbits by the east gate.
When Jade Sung aided King of Hsiang,

He could compose his *Verse to T'ang*.
Tune of Green Water I oft hear;
I'm lucky to have heard it here.
Now it clears up, so blue the sky;
The haze has gone with the mist by.
The phoenix's plumes brightly sheen
As it perches upon Mt. Queen.
From northwest blows a wind so high;
To South Sea the phoenix does fly.
When young I had all means well planned,
Favored by the Lord, kind and grand.
As white jade is stained by green flies,
No friendship between the peers lies.
One ought to do as is required;
A holy heart is most admired.
When can Mid-plain be a pure place
So that we could repay His grace?

* Ch'in: the Ch'in State or the State of Ch'in (905 B.C.- 206 B.C.), enfeoffed as a dependency of Chough by King Piety of Chough in 905 B.C. and enfeoffed as a vassal state by King Peace of Chough in 770 B.C. In the ten years from 230 B.C. to 221 B.C., Ch'in wiped out the other six powers and became the first unified regime of China, i.e., the Ch'in Empire.
* Ssu Li (284 B.C.- 208 B.C.): a renowned statesman, litterateur and calligrapher, whose political ideas have had a profound impact on China and laid the foundation of China's political system for more than two thousand years. After Emperor First of Ch'in died, Ssu was given a death sentence due to a false accusation. Before his execution, he sighed to his son that it would be impossible to hunt anymore.
* Jade Sung: Jade Sung (cir. 298 B.C.- cir. 222 B.C.), a student of Yüan Ch'ü's. In the myths, King Huai of Ch'u once met a girl and had an intercourse overnight in his dream. Jade Sung recorded the story in Verse to T'ang when he traveled with King Hsiang to Mt. Witch.
* *Verse to T'ang*: a verse composed by Jade Sung, a student of Yüan Ch'ü's, a poet from

the State of Ch'u.
* Tune of Green Water: one of the lyric tunes played by singers and a subgenre or theme adopted by poets to write on to go with the ready tune.
* Mt. Queen: or Mt. Kunlun if transliterated, is the most sacred mountain in China. It starts from the Eastern Pamir Plateau, stretches across New Land (Hsinchiang) and Tibet, and extends to Ch'inghai, with an average altitude of 5,500 – 6,000 meters. In Chinese myths, Mt. Queen is where Mother West dwells.
* South Sea: what is now South China Sea.

戏赠郑溧阳

陶令日日醉，
不知五柳春。
素琴本无弦，
漉酒用葛巾。
清风北窗下，
自谓羲皇人。
何时到栗里，
一见平生亲。

To Cheng, Magistrate of Lishine for Fun

Poolbright is drunk day after day,
Not seeing the spring, his willows sway.
There are no strings on lutes like that;
Wine is filtered with his hemp hat.
There to the window blows a breeze;
He says he's Hidden Spirit at ease.
When could I come to Lishine to stay
So that with my friend I could play?

* Lishine: a town in present-day Changchow, Chiangsu Province.
* Poolbright: Ch'ien T'ao or Yüanming Tao (A.D. 352 – A.D. 427) if transliterated, a complex figure and a poet of complex poems—a verse writer, poet, and litterateur in the Chin dynasty, and the founder of Chinese idyllism, who was once the magistrate of P'engtse.
* Wine is filtered with his hemp hat: Poolbright loved wine so much that he would filter wine with his hat and then put on the hat soaked with wine.

* hemp: a tall annual Asian herb (Gannabis sativa) of the mulberry family, with small green flowers and a tough bark, the fibers from which are used for cloth and cordage.
* Hidden Spirit: Fuhsi if transliterated, the ancestor of Chinese, the earliest documented god of creation and king of kings in Chinese culture. Sky Water (T'ienshui) in today's Kansu Province is believed to be Hidden Spirit's birthplace, as is the topographical center of China.

赠僧崖公

昔在朗陵东，
学禅白眉空。
大地了镜彻，
回旋寄轮风。
揽彼造化力，
持为我神通。
晚谒泰山君，
亲见日没云。
夜卧雪上月，
拂衣逃人群。
授余金仙道，
旷劫未始闻。
冥机发天光，
独朗谢垢氛。
虚舟不系物，
观化游江濆。
江濆遇同声，
道崖乃僧英。
说法动海岳，
游方化公卿。
手秉玉麈尾，
如登白楼亭。
微言注百川，
亹亹信可听。
一风鼓群有，
万籁各自鸣。
启闭八窗牖，

托宿挈电霆。
自言历天台,
搏壁蹑翠屏。
凌兢石桥去,
恍惚入青冥。
昔往今来归,
绝景无不经。
何日更携手,
乘杯向蓬瀛?

To Monk Cliff

Before, I learned Zen from White Brow
In what is called the Light Hills now.
The earth transparent you could feel,
Turning, leaning on the Cloud Wheel.
I drew on his chemical force
That did turn into my resource.
I visited Mt. Arch at night,
When the sun went behind clouds white.
I slept on snow with moonlight spread;
Away from the crowd I had fled.
He taught me the Way of Gold Ore
That I had never heard before.
From what was unseen shot a glow,
Free of all dust and pure like snow.
My body not moored like a boat,
Upon an ocean there, afloat.
I met a friend by the spring brink,
Who said that Word Cliff was the pink.

His teaching seas and mounts did quake;
His preaching lords and peers did shake.
He took a dusting broom in hand
As if on a cloud he did stand.
His words flowed like a river clear,
Refreshing, pleasant to the ear.
Like wind urging things all around,
Each sound reproducing a sound.
The eight windows were opened wide;
At lightning you seemed to abide.
You said to Mt. Heaven you'd been,
Climbing up a cliff like a screen.
With care, the stone bridge you went thru,
As if having merged with the blue.
Time goes on from the past to now;
Good scenes you have enjoyed enow.
When could we go hand in hand
Once more by cup to Fairyland?

* Zen: a kind of performance of quietude in a form of meditation or contemplation. When Sanskrit jana was introduced to China, it was translated as Zan or Zen for this kind of practice. In the T'ang dynasty, educated Chinese were imbued with Zen, and many of them were associated with Zen monks and spent much time in Zen monasteries.
* White Brow: unidentified, probably a Buddhist.
* the Cloud Wheel: a term reflecting Buddhist cosmology. In Buddhism, the first layer of a world is called the Cloud Wheel. What beyond the Cloud Wheel is a layer of water called the Water Wheel, and what beyond the Water Wheel is a layer of rock called the Metal Wheel which carries mountains, seas and lands.
* Mt. Arch: the first of the Five Mountains in China, located in today's Shantung Province, the highest in East China and the most honored, the other four mountains being Mt. Ever in Shanhsi, Mt. Scale in Hunan, Mt. Flora in Sha'anhsi, and Mt. Tower in Honan.

* the Way of Gold Ore: Gold Ore indicates Buddha.
* Mt. Heaven: different from the other Mt. Heaven, this mountain is the birthplace of Heaven sect of Chinese Buddhism and southern sect of Wordism, located in present-day Chechiang Province.
* Fairyland: referring to the fairy mountains in East Sea.

游溧阳北湖亭望瓦屋山怀古赠同旅

朝登北湖亭,
遥望瓦屋山。
天清白露下,
始觉秋风还。
游子托主人,
仰观眉睫间。
目色送飞鸿,
邈然不可攀。
长吁相劝勉,
何事来吴关?
闻有贞义女,
振穷溧水湾。
清光了在眼,
白日如披颜。
高坟五六墩,
崒兀栖猛虎。
遗迹翳九泉,
芳名动千古。
子胥昔乞食,
此女倾壶浆。
运开展宿愤,
入楚鞭平王。
凛冽天地间,
闻名若怀霜。
壮夫或未达,
十步九太行。
与君拂衣去,

万里同翱翔。

To My Vagrant Partner at the Kiosk North of Lishine Lake While Taking a View of Mt. Tiles

The kiosk at dawn north of the lake,
A far view of Mt. Tiles I take.
The ground is spread with frosty dew;
I feel an autumn wind back blow.
A vagrant who feels low and down
Is well aware of his host's frown.
Just like seeing off the wild geese,
This host looks aloof and he is.
The vagrant to calm himself sighs:
Why should be here, wherefores and whys?
Once there was a chaste girl I hear,
Who saved Wu out of water there.
Her glamour his eyes did beguile;
The sun seemed to bloom with a smile.
Her tomb is about five tombs high,
As if a tiger lives thereby.
Her body is there down below,
Moving heroes who come and go.
Wu begged from this girl some food;
She gave him as much as she could.
Wu rose and took revenge in Ch'u,
Whipping King Peace's body thru.
She's noble between earth and sky,
Her name lingers on, pure and high.

When a gallant has no right time,
Each step, Mt. Great Go he will climb.
Let's go ahead, worry no more;
Across the boundless sky we soar.

* Lishine: a town located in the Yangtze River Delta, in present-day Ch'angchow, Chiangsu Province.
* Mt. Tiles: a mountain 40 kilometers northwest of Lishine County.
* wild goose: an undomesticated goose that is caring and responsible, taken as a symbol of benevolence, righteousness, good manner, wisdom, and faith in Chinese culture.
* Wu: referring to Tzuhsu Wu (559 B.C.- 484 B.C.), a renowned minister of Wu. In 522 B.C., Tzuhsu Wu escaped from Ch'u when his father and elder brother were killed by King Peace. He begged a chaste girl at Lishine for food and repeatedly asked her not to tell anyone where he was. To assure Tzuhsu Wu and keep to her words, the girl carried a rock on her back and drowned herself.
* Ch'u: a big vassal state of Chough, one of the powers in the Warring States period, conquered and annexed by Ch'in in 223 B.C.
* King Peace: King Peace of Ch'u (? - 516 B.C.), a king of Ch'u in the Spring and Autumn period.
* Mt. Great Go: Mt. T'aihang if transliterated, meandering on the border of Shanhsi, Honan and Sha'anhsi, an important mountain range in East China and a geographic watershed.

醉后赠从甥高镇

马上相逢揖马鞭，
客中相见客中怜。
欲邀击筑悲歌饮，
正值倾家无酒钱。
江东风光不借人，
枉杀落花空自春。
黄金逐手快意尽，
昨日破产今朝贫。
丈夫何事空啸傲，
不如烧却头上巾。
君为进士不得进，
我被秋霜生旅鬓。
时清不及英豪人，
三尺童儿重廉蔺。
匣中盘剑装鲳鱼，
闲在腰间未用渠。
且将换酒与君醉，
醉归托宿吴专诸。

To Chen Kao, My Nephew, When I'm Drunk

Of our horse astride, each other we greet;
In this land adrift, each other we meet.
Plucking the *quin*, for a drink I would whine;
So broke, I have no more money for wine.

In this south land you can't borrow an air;
Spring comes in vain and blooms fall in despair.
Not poor, I have squandered my gold away;
Going bankrupt yesterday, I'm poor today.
Why the hell should a brave man in vain shout?
He should have thrown his hat and burned it out.
Grand Test you failed and your future you've lost;
And the autumn has touched my hair with frost.
With peaceful time swordsmen do not fit in;
Even striplings well respect Lien and Lin.
My sword in the shark skin sheath on my waist,
No use at all for it, my sword lies waste.
Exchange it for wine, I'll get drunk with you;
Drunk, we go and sleep in Chuan's house in Wu.

* *quin*: an ancient Chinese musical instrument with five strings like a quinton. It was played by plucking the strings while the player sang and drank.
* Grand Test: also called Court Test or Court Examination, the highest level of the civil-service examinations aiming at selecting qualified officials, instituted by Emperor Highsire of T'ang (A.D. 628 - A.D.683), held every three years and the final decision of ranking was made by an emperor himself.
* Lien and Lin: referring to P'o Lien, a renowned commander of Chao, and Hsiangju Lin, a renowned statesman and diplomat of Chao.
* Chuan: referring to Chuan Chu, one of the Four Assassins in Chinese history living in the Spring and Autumn period. He hid his knife in a fish and killed the king of Wu while he was serving him fish.

赠秋浦柳少府

秋浦旧萧索，
公庭人吏稀。
因君树桃李，
此地忽芳菲。
摇笔望白云，
开帘当翠微。
时来引山月，
纵酒酣清晖。
而我爱夫子，
淹留未忍归。

To Liu, a County Sheriff of Autumn Shore

Autumn Shore was so bleak before;
Just very few officials one saw.
You've come and brought about a boom;
All trees and grass make haste to bloom.
Taking your brush, at clouds you peer;
Drawing the shade, you find green leer.
The night ushers in the moon bright;
You propose a toast to her light.
How I love you, I love you dear;
I would not go back home from here!

* Autumn Shore: southwest of today's Kuich'ih County, Anhui Province, rich in silver and copper resources.

* brush: any of various writing brushes or called Chinese brush, widely used for writing or painting, invented or renovated by Tien Meng (259 B.C.- 210 B.C.), a general in the Ch'in dynasty.
* the moon: the celestial body that revolves around the earth from west to east as a satellite, which appears at night and gives off shining silvery light, an image of purity and solitude in Chinese culture.

赠崔秋浦三首

To Ts'ui, Magistrate of Autumn Shore, Three Poems

其 一

吾爱崔秋浦，
宛然陶令风。
门前五杨柳，
井上二梧桐。
山鸟下厅事，
檐花落酒中。
怀君未忍去，
惆怅意无穷。

No. 1

I love Ts'ui, Head of Autumn Shore,
Like Ch'ien T'ao, whose glee all adore.
Five willows wave before his hall;
Two phoenix trees well-side grow tall.
In front of the hall birds alight;
Into the wine fall petals bright.
Loving you, I won't go away;
Feeling lonely, I'd longer stay.

* Phoenix Tree: Chinese parasol tree, so named because phoenixes perch on Chinese parasol trees.
* Ch'ien T'ao: referring to Poolbright T'ao (A.D. 352 – A.D. 427), a verse writer, poet, and litterateur in the Chin dynasty, and the founder of Chinese idyllism, who was once

the magistrate of P'engtse. Pure and lofty, T'ao resigned from official life several times to live a life of simplicity. There were five willow trees planted in front of his house, so he called himself Mr. Five Willows.

其 二

崔令学陶令，
北窗常昼眠。
抱琴时弄月，
取意任无弦。
见客但倾酒，
为官不爱钱。
东皋春事起，
种黍早归田。

No. 2

Magistrate learns from Magistrate;
Near the sunlit sill he sleeps late.
With his lute the moon he would play;
Interesting, have no strings it may.
To his guest a cup he'll uphold;
An official is not for gold.
East there, spring farming must be done;
Go there and sow millet anon.

* Magistrate learns from Magistrate: the first Magistrate refers to Pai Li's friend, Ts'ui, who was the magistrate of Autumn Shore; the second Magistrate refers to Poolbright T'ao, who was once the magistrate of P'engtse.
* the moon: the planet of the earth, which appears at night and gives off shining silvery light, an image of purity and solitude in Chinese culture.
* millet: a member of the foxtail grass family, or its seeds, cultivated as a cereal, used as a stable food in ancient times, having been cultivated in China for more than 7,300 years, one of the earliest crops in the world.

其 三

河阳花作县，
秋浦玉为人。
地逐名贤好，
风随惠化春。
水从天汉落，
山逼画屏新。
应念金门客，
投沙吊楚臣。

No. 3

In Rivershine, the clime's a bloom
In Autumn Shore, the jade's a groom.
The place for its gents has its name;
The folks for their boon have their fame.
Water falls from the Milky Way;
Mountains like a new screen there stay.
I, a lone guest from Golden Gate,
Come to worship Ch'ü Yüan, the great.

* Rivershine: a county in Yangchow, Huainan See in the T'ang dynasty.
* Autumn Shore: southwest of today's Kuich'ih County, Anhui Province, rich in silver and copper resources.
* the Milky Way: the Silver River in Chinese mythology, a luminous band circling the heavens composed of stars and nebulae; the Galaxy. As legend goes, the Milky Way maid, the granddaughter of Emperor of Heaven fell in love with a worldly cowherd and they gave birth to a son and a daughter. When their love was disclosed to Emperor of Heaven, he sent Queen Mother to take the fairy back to Heaven. While Cowherd was trying to catch up in a boat the cow had made with its horn broken, Queen Mother

望九华赠青阳韦仲堪

昔在九江上，
遥望九华峰。
天河挂绿水，
秀出九芙蓉。
我欲一挥手，
谁人可相从。
君为东道主，
于此卧云松。

To Chungk'an Wei, Magistrate of Blueshine While Looking at Mt. Nine Flowers

Then, the Nine Rivers saw me oar;
And gazing, Mt. Nine Flowers I looked for.
Blueness hung from the Milky Way;
Nine Lotus Flowers revealed did sway.
I'd raise my hand to greet the sough;
Who'll follow me up to play now?
O my friend, here you are the host;
You rest neath the pine tree, reposed.

* the Nine Rivers: Bankshine, today's Chiuchiang, Chianghsi Province or the nine rivers in this area, after which the city was named.
* Mt. Nine Flowers: one of the Four Buddhist Mountains in China in present-day Anhui Province, on which nine peaks look like nine lotus flowers.
* the Milky Way: also known as the Silver River in Chinese mythology, a luminous band circling the heavens composed of stars and nebulae indistinguishable to the naked eye; the Galaxy.

rived the air with her hairpin, so there appeared the Silver River, i.e., the Milky Way to keep them apart, and the fairy and the cowherd became two stars called Vega and Altair.

* Golden Gate: a palace gate near the national academy in the T'ang dynasty.
* Yüan Ch'ü: Yüan Ch'ü (340 B.C.- 278 B.C.), a great patriotic poet and high official of Ch'u, who threw himself into a river, so aggrieved at his broken state.